Diary of

a

Wizard Kid

1 & 2

by

Boyd Brent

Contact: boyd.brent1@gmail.com

Diary of

a

Wizard Kid

by

Boyd Brent

Diary of a Wizard Kid

Okay. I know what you must be thinking. But I'm not *that* guy. My name doesn't even rhyme with rotter. It's Jimmy Drummer. And all I've got in common with that guy is we're both wizards. I mean, I didn't even want to be a wizard. Anyway, I got to thinking, there must be a world of kids out there who think going to wizard school over in England would be super cool. Well, if you're one of those kids, I've got three words for you right off the bat: 'pointy hat' and 'broomstick'. You ever caught a reflection of yourself sweeping a classroom in a pointy hat? It's no joke I can tell you. You *still* think being a wizard would be cool? Well, stick around because you haven't heard nothing yet. No word of a lie, you're about to experience the craziest adventure a regular dude has EVER had ...

Wednesday (the day it all happened)

So like I was saying, I was just your average 11-year-old dude. Which is all I ever wanted to be (until I turned 12). But, oh no! That was, like, *too much* to ask. Man, it's not like I even *believed* in dumb magic. Anyway, I was in the mall recently. Just mooching about. Sucking on a popsicle. Minding my own. When I noticed this strange dude wearing a top hat and leaning on an umbrella. He looked like Mary Poppins's brother or something. Then the dude winked at me. You heard me right. *Winked*. Man, I tried *real* hard not to look at him. But you probably know what it's like when you try not to look at someone – the more you try the more you stare right at them. And that's when he tapped the end of his nose like we shared a big secret. I figured this was a pretty serious situation. So I slid off my stool and made a bee line for the exit. And *that's* when my world changed forever. The guy started swinging his umbrella and everyone, and I mean *everyone*, got frozen where they stood. "What ho, young man!" he said, in the happiest, dumbest English accent you've ever heard in your whole life. I bet you're thinking that if you found yourself in a situation like that you'd be all cool about it. Maybe say something like, 'Oh, hey there English dude! Neat trick swinging your umbrella and turning everyone in the mall into mannequins.' Well, I've got news for you: there's *no way* you would have said that. You'd have yelled something like, "This SHOULD NOT be happening to a regular dude!" just like I did. So anyway, the guy started to twirl his moustache (did I mention he had a moustache? Well he did. And it curled up at each end.) So he's twirling his moustache with one hand and swinging his umbrella with the other when he said, "No need to look so alarmed, old bean." That's right. He called me an 'old bean.' Then he swung the pointy end of his umbrella right into my knee. Okay, it was an accident. I know that now. The dude is just seriously accident prone. But at the time I didn't know that. How could I? I thought maybe he was crazy enough to think I *was* an old bean. And maybe he hated old beans and went travelling

5

through space and time attacking them with his umbrella. So I told him, "I'm not old, mister! And do I *look* like a vegetable to you? Seriously, dude!" Anyway, I wanted to make a run for it but I couldn't 'cos my knee was killing me. So I made a hop for it. And no word of a lie, he hopped right alongside me. "Now listen here," he said, "I've got something jolly important to tell you."

"Go away!" I told him.

"You're a little confused I can tell. But I can explain it all in a jiffy."

"You deaf or something? Go away! You got the wrong guy!"

"You are Jimmy Drummer are you not?"

"Yeah. No! Whatever! Just leave me alone, dude!"

"I'm afraid I can't. Not if you're Jimmy Drummer of 6 Little Hamlet Street, Ft Myers, Florida, USA."

"How'd you find out where I live?!"

"It's my job to know all about you. What I don't know about you Jimmy Drummer of 6 Little Hamlet Street, Ft Myers, Florida, could fit on the back of a postage stamp."

"You need help, mister! You really do!" That's when he froze me mid hop. So I'm suspended like a foot off the ground. And the only things I could move were my lips. I found that out when I mumbled, "Now this here should *defo* not be happening to a regular dude."

"You, regular? Stuff and nonsense," he said. "You're about as far from regular as a four headed toad shopping for a toaster at a garage sale. Or a cat with eleven lives and eight legs dancing a tango with a purple rhinoceros. In fact, it could be said that you're about as regular as ..."

"Okay," I mumbled. "Stop with the dumb comparisons. I get it. I'm a freak. Just unfreeze me already."

"Well, maybe I will. But only if you stop *hopping about* and hear me out."

"I wasn't hopping about, mister. What kind of an idiot do you take me for? I was *hopping away* … away from you 'cos you're really wigging me out," I mumbled.

"Well, I'll only unfreeze you if you'll give me your word that you'll stop trying to hop off – and you might as well because I hold the British hopping record – so your chances of escape are about as remote as a spot of bother in the middle of a sponge pudding. And that's pretty darned remote I can tell you."

"I have no idea what you just told me, mister. But I'll hear you out," I mumbled.

"You mean it, old bean?"

"Yes. I mean it." So he unfroze me and I made a dash for it. But he snagged my foot with his umbrella and I hit the deck and slid a ways on the polished floor. "I say, that wasn't very sportsman-like. You know, for someone with extraordinary powers who's destined to fight the forces of evil, you seem awfully accident prone."

"*What* did you just say? I'm SO NOT destined to fight the forces of evil! I'm just a regular guy who's gonna be a surfer dude or maybe get a job in the mall!"

"You SO ARE destined to fight the forces of evil. You really don't have the first clue about your extraordinary powers. Do you, old scone?" That's right, he called me an old scone that time. I'd had enough. I really had. So I stood up and looked him right in the eyes. "Look man, there's no way I've got any powers! You got that?"

"That's where you're wrong. You, my dear boy, are a wizard of the first order," he said, leaning on his umbrella and smiling.

"I'm a *what*? You're crazy. There's no such thing as wizards. They only exist in books, dude."

"Well, I'll let you into a little secret," he said. Then he looked over his shoulder like he didn't want any of those people he just froze to hear. "This *is* a book," he said.

"You need help, mister. You really do. This is my life."

"Yes, it's your life, but … it's also a book. And what's more, someone is reading this book right now."

"*Who's* reading it?"

"That I couldn't tell you. But reading it they are. Right now."

Listen, you must know who you are reading this right now. Which means you know something this guy didn't. So you might want to pat yourself on the back or something. Anyway, I told him, "Look man, I *know* I don't have any powers. I mean, my last school report said 'Jimmy's going to be a *total* drop-out unless he tries a LOT harder'. Does that *sound* like someone with extraordinary powers to you?"

"You do have them. And I'm certain that when you see what you've been doing with your extraordinary powers," he said, shaking a finger right in my face, "you'll realise how important it is that you learn how to control them." Right then this bubble appeared and I could see myself walking down my street inside it. I jumped a little. Then I asked him, "How are you *doing this*?"

"No time to explain now, old sport. The spell I cast on this shopping parade is due to wear off any time. So look and learn my boy, look and learn ..."

So I looked, but I didn't expect to learn much. "Look, man," I said, "I knew I could walk down my street already. It's no biggie. I do it all the time. All I have to do is leave my house and put one foot in front of the other."

"Maybe so. Maybe so. But look how you just turned the corner into Adams Avenue ..."

"I knew I could do that too. All I have to do is follow the bend in the road ..."

"And right now," he said, "unless I'm very much mistaken, you're about to tell the young fellow who lives at number 30 to 'go take a flying leap.'"

"Yeah? What of it? That little dude's been bugging me for weeks. Every time I walk past his house he starts singing 'cos this one time I told him to put a sock in it."

"The fact that he sings like a porcupine with nappy rash is neither here nor there. Just look what happens the second you turn the corner."

"I know what happens. He stopped singing and started yelling about something."

"Yes ... but would you like to know *why* he started yelling?"

"Not really. Kids are always yelling. I thought maybe he stubbed a toe or something. Who cares?"

"Oh, you thought he stubbed a toe, did you? Well, look and learn my boy, look and learn ..." I knew the deal when it came to looking and learning with this dude. So far I'd looked and learned nothing. So I told him, "What*ever*," and looked into his bubble. And that's when I saw the kid at number 30 take an *actual* flying leap like I'd just told him to do ... right onto the roof of his house. He was hanging from the guttering by his fingertips. And for some reason he was yelling like he'd just stubbed his toe. "I *did* that?" I said.

"Yes, you jolly well did. And that's just one of many things you've been doing of late." So right then the bubble burst. "So what happened next? Did the little guy fall off his roof!?"

"Well, actually, yes, yes he did. But thanks to Montgomery

Kensington here, who caught the little blighter, he'll live to sing like a flatulent porcupine another day."

So anyway, Montgomery Kensington (yes, that's what his folks actually called him) showed me a bunch of other stuff I'd been doing to people without knowing it. And then he said, "You, my dear fellow, are a danger to man and beast alike." So I told the dude I didn't want *any part* of being a person with extraordinary powers. And he said I didn't have a choice. That my extraordinary powers weren't about to go anywhere. That I was ... how did he put it? Oh, yeah, "Bally well stuck with my extraordinary powers whether I liked it or not." Then he told me he had important bits and bobs to attend to and he couldn't follow me around making sure I didn't wipe out half the neighborhood for the rest of his life. Man, it really seemed like I had no choice – I wouldn't be going to Edison High next semester. Instead, I'd be going to some wizard school over in England. Montgomery Kensington drew me a picture of it. Like *that* was supposed to cheer me up. It's the one on the front cover of my diary. Man, all this was all happening so fast my head was spinning. It really was.

20 minutes later ...

I went over to my best friend's house to get some stuff off my chest. My best friend's name is Andy. So Andy opened his front door, "Hey, dude. Why the long face? Your folks find out you've been skipping school to catch some waves, surfer dude?"

"It's way worse than that," I said. "Trust me, man, nothing is *ever* gonna be the same again."

"You better come in then," he said.

So we go up to his room where he's playing his favourite video game: *Man Eating Monsters From Planet Neutron*. Right away he unpaused the action and started blasting those man-eaters. "So what's the deal?" he asked. I didn't feel much like beating around the bush. So I just came right out with it. "Look," I said, "I've got something pretty weird to tell you."

"Shoot," he said, shooting.

"It doesn't look like I'll be starting Edison High with you after all." Andy threw down his game controller so hard it bounced six feet in the air. "*What?*" he said. "No way, dude! I hate you! And now I'm gonna make you pay for this BIG TIME!" No, Andy wasn't talking to me. He was talking to the boss monster who'd just crushed his head with a rock. Then he sat down and looked at me like he couldn't believe his ears. "*What* did you just say?"

"I said it doesn't look like I'll be going to Edison High next semester, Andy. Sorry, dude."

"Are your folks moving out of town or something?"

"No. It's like this ... I have to go to wizard school over in England and learn to control my extraordinary powers." You have *no idea* how dumb I felt saying that. Don't believe me? Then try saying it to your best friend and see how dumb you feel.

"Funny guy," said Andy, pushing the replay button.

"It's true, dude. It really is."

"Yeah. And I'll be starting my new job as a line backer for the Chicago Bulls."

"Look, man, I just found out I got some extraordinary powers. And I need to learn how to control them ASAP. I know it sounds crazy. But I've been making kids take *actual* flying leaps and a whole bunch of other crazy stuff that I don't want to get into 'cos it's too depressing."

"... man, *you're* crazy. I mean, if *you* have extraordinary powers, then *I* can get inside this TV and blast this monster boss for real." Right then it kinda felt like maybe anything was possible. So I said, "Who knows, maybe you *can* get inside your TV, Andy ..." That's when Andy vanished. I sat up to attention so fast my head snapped back. "Andy!" I called out. "Andy! Stop kidding around, man!" That's when Andy's face popped up inside his TV. And that monster boss was due in 5, 4, 3, 2, 1 seconds ...

I guessed by the way Andy had gone all bug-eyed that he could hear that countdown too. And then the monster boss appeared on the horizon behind Andy. So I jumped up and pointed. "Andy! Run, man! Run!" It felt like the least I could do. Anyway, I never saw a kid run as fast as Andy did before or since. I felt pretty lousy about what had happened. I really did. And I knew I had to get Andy out of his TV before that boss monster hit him with the rock he was carrying. So I reminded myself that I had extraordinary powers. *You've got extraordinary powers*, I thought, *and now would be a good time to use them*! "Abracadabra! I want Andy back in this room! Right now!" Nothing. "... Hocus pocus! Get Andy back here now!" Nothing. I knelt down in front of Andy's TV but there was no sign of him in there. Or that boss monster. I was really starting to sweat. And then Montgomery Kensington appeared on the horizon. Man, I never thought I'd be so pleased to spot an English weirdo on TV. So Montgomery Kensington runs out of shot. Then he runs back into shot carrying Andy under his arm. Andy sure looked spooked. So Montgomery Kensington waved his finger at me and then he darted out of shot again. Then the boss monster flew in shot holding that rock over his head and grinning ... and then he flew out of shot in the direction of Montgomery Kensington. I figured this was getting kinda interesting. So I pulled up a chair and sat down. I'd just got comfortable when Montgomery Kensington runs back into shot, carrying Andy under his other arm. Man, Andy still looked *totally* freaked. Then Montgomery Kensington waved a finger at me again before he ran out of shot again. And the boss monster ran into shot with an even bigger rock ... and then out of shot in the direction of Montgomery Kensington. Anyway, this went on for some time. I was about to open a packet of Andy's potato chips when Andy flew out the TV and landed on his bed. So Andy sat there staring at me with that same bug-eyed look that he'd had for the last ten minutes. Then he cleared his throat and said, "So when are you leaving for wizard school, dude?" He even offered to help me pack.

1 hour later ...

Montgomery Kensington stopped by my house to explain everything to my dad. My dad's a builder. He drives a pick-up truck. He's a no-nonsense type of guy. I know for sure he's a no-nonsense type of guy 'cos he tells me on a regular basis. And then he says, "So NO MORE NONSENSE, okay?" Man, my stomach was in knots. I didn't even want to *think* about what a no-nonsense guy like Dad would make of Montgomery Kensington. It was like every word that dude said sounded like nonsense. Mom was away visiting my aunty Pam. But as I explained to Montgomery Kensington, Mom trusts Dad's judgement. So if he thinks it's cool that I go to wizard school over in England, then she's sure to agree. So anyway, my dad was out front loading bricks onto the back of his truck when Montgomery Kensington pulled up in a yellow Rolls Royce. A big ol' convertible that looked like an antique. So my dad was lifting bricks onto the back of his truck when Montgomery Kensington shouted, "What ho, old fruit!" I guess Dad wasn't expecting someone to call him an old fruit. Not ever in his whole life. So that explains why he dropped a brick on his foot. I never thought I'd hear my dad scream that loud neither. So Montgomery Kensington jumped out of his Rolls Royce. "My my, we are accident-prone today, what-what?" he told Dad. "Let me take a look at that foot. I'll have you know I have a certificate in first aid, what-what?" I guess that's when Montgomery Kensington grabbed Dad's foot and Dad lost his balance and fell on his backside. I can't tell you what Dad told Montgomery Kensington then. But it seemed pretty clear that Montgomery Kensington had never been called those words before. "Now, I say! I've come over here with nothing but kindness and the spirit of goodwill towards all men in my heart. To tell you I think your son is extraordinary and that I want to take him back to England with me. And you call me a ..." I can't tell you what Montgomery Kensington said to Dad. But it sure did sound odd him saying it. Dad must've got the idea in his head that the dude was dangerous, because right then he yelled for me to go to my room and lock the door. I was already in my room, watching from my bedroom window and thinking this probably could have gone better. So Dad got up and hopped after Montgomery Kensington with a spade. And Montgomery Kensington hopped away from him. Well, he didn't so much hop *away* as round and round my front yard in circles. "Hopping must be in the Drummer blood," Montgomery Kensington said to Dad, "but as I told your son earlier today, I've been the British hopping champion for four years in a row. And as hard as your son tried – and believe me he tried *bally* hard – he couldn't hop away from me. So the chances of you catching me in a hop are as about as remote as a flea on an elephant's fat hairy bottom." That's when Dad shouted for someone to call the police. So I ran downstairs and out into the back yard. "I think I need this guy's help, Dad!" And that's when Montgomery Kensington froze my dad mid-hop. It sure was weird seeing a no-nonsense guy like Dad frozen like that. "Sorry, old bean," Montgomery Kensington said, "but drastic times call for drastic measures." So I waved a hand in front of Dad's face. Nothing. "Have you killed my father?" I asked.

"Killed him? Of course I haven't killed him. He's sleeping more soundly than a babe following a hearty meal of roast beef and Yorkshire puddings."

"So what now?" I said, crouching down and waving my hand in the space between Dad's floaty feet and the ground they normally stood on. "Well, it seems to me your father is not a man easily impressed by reason. So I think a spell will be just the ticket to make him more ... what's the word I'm looking for?"

"Reasonable," I suggested.

"Clever lad."

"What kind of a spell? I can't let you mess up my dad's head."

"Well ... the spell I have in mind is a bit like a baking spell."

"I can't let you bake my dad," I said.

"Oh, come now. It's quite harmless. Just think of your father as a cake. And me as the chef who'll be adding a few ingredients to the cake to make it more reasonable. Your father will then agree with whatever a certain fellow called Montgomery Kensington tells him."

"I guess that will be okay," I said. So he went and got a wand from the glove box of his car. "No need to look like a hungry squirrel who's forgotten where he left his nuts, old fruit. I use this little spell on people all the time. You'd be amazed by how many unreasonable people I encounter on my travels."

"No, I wouldn't," I said. So then he tapped my dad on his head with his wand twice.

And then, "Once for luck." So Dad floated down onto his feet and opened his eyes. And it was like he'd forgotten everything that went on since Montgomery Kensington arrived. "My name is Montgomery Kensington. It's jolly nice to meet you, old chap," he tells Dad.

"Good to meet you too, fella," said Dad. "What can I do for you?"

"It's more what I can do for you. Or more specifically, your boy here. I'm going to take him over to England to a great school where they'll help him master his extraordinary powers. How does that sound?"

"It sounds just swell," said Dad, smiling and shaking Montgomery Kensington's hand. "We'll be off, then," said Montgomery Kensington, grabbing my arm and leading me towards his car.

"*What*?" I said. "Just like *that*? Shouldn't I go pack a bag or something?"

"Not really necessary, old bean. They'll have everything you need in Ye Olde Shoppe of Magic'." Then he got in the passenger seat of his car and patted the driver's seat like he expected me to drive.

"First off," I said, "I don't have any money to buy stuff in Ye Olde Shoppe of Magic, and second … I can't drive this thing 'cos I'm 11 years old and I haven't got a licence, dude!" Montgomery Kensington just stared at me like I was talking some language he didn't understand. So Dad walked over and I figured he was gonna put the dude straight on a few things. But Dad just opened his wallet and asked me how much money I needed to buy stuff at Ye Olde Shoppe of Magic. Montgomery Kensington told him that wouldn't be necessary because they don't except money. "Only Wizard Credits," he told him. Then Dad opened the driver's door and shoved me into the seat. "But, Dad ..." I said.

"It's okay, son. Just don't go getting the gas and brake pedals mixed up and you'll be fine."

"But Dad … aren't you forgetting something?" I thought he was going to say, "Oh yeah! What was I thinking? You haven't passed your driving test. And you're 11 years old." But all he said was, "Quite right, son. Put your seat belt on." Then he looked around inside the car, but couldn't find a seat belt 'cos they hadn't been *invented* when they made that car. So Dad said, "No seatbelts? Not a problem, son. Just hold on tight and you'll be fine." Then he patted my shoulder and stepped away from the car. So Montgomery Kensington told me to close my mouth unless I wanted to catch flies in it. And that's when we took off. And I mean straight up in the air like a helicopter! Man, if you were in a Rolls Royce that shot up in the air and you looked down and saw your house was the size of a *matchbox* you probably think you'd say something cool like, "Love the flying car, dude! So what's the 0-60 like on this thing, anyway?" Well, if you think you would've said that, I've got news for you. There's no way you would have said that. You'd have said something like, "For the love of computer games! I don't know how to fly this thing! And another thing ... I'm way to regular a dude to die like this!" just like I did.

Some time later ...

I can't really tell you much about what I saw on that journey. My eyes were shut for most of it. And I'd put my fingers in my ears because Montgomery Kensington was driving me nuts. And in case you were wondering, he was flying the car with his moustache. No word of a lie. When he tugged the left side of his moustache, the car turned to the right. And when he tugged the right side of his moustache, the car turned to the left. Apparently it works that way to confuse robbers if they ever steal his car. But that would mean they'd need his moustache to fly the car. And it seemed unlikely they'd have his moustache because it's stuck to his face. I guess I put my fingers in my ears when he tried to explain. I couldn't cope. I really couldn't. Anyway, I felt the muscles in my face start to bristle like a fighter pilot when he hits g-force. So I opened one eye and saw clouds and stars whizzing past at warp speed. And that's when I saw it for the first time: Skyforest Wizard School. Man, it's impossible to tell from that picture on the front of my diary just how big and old and scary-looking Skyforest Wizard School actually is. As we got closer, I could see towers and turrets and MASSIVE chimneys with smoke coming out of them. So Montgomery Kensington tells me to close my mouth again, "Unless you intend to catch flies in it," he said. And then he said he had some good news for me. But I guess his idea of good news and mine are pretty different. "The good news is," he tells me, "that the flies in Skyforest are too fat to swallow. So the blighters just get wedged in any mouth they buzz into." Man, I closed my mouth so fast I maybe cracked a tooth. That explains why I was rubbing my jaw when Montgomery Kensington landed the car.

You ever followed a crazy English dude through a big ol' haunted-looking wizard school? Well, I have. And it's seriously weird. And not in a good way. "Where are all the kids?" I asked.

"They're on holiday until next week," he told me.

"So why the big rush to bring me here?"

"Patience, old fruit. All will be revealed in the fullness of time."

So we climbed up this twisty staircase. Man, that staircase seemed to go on for*ever.* My legs were smarting when we finally reached the top. And then we walked down this long corridor with kids' dormitories all the way along it. Montgomery Kensington opened a door right at the end. "This is your dorm. Your home away from home. Your little wizard's nest high above the enchanted forest. And what's more, the views of the enchanted forest from the windows of this room are second to none." So I went up to this window and stood there taking in the views. If I'm honest, the enchanted forest looked more scary than enchanting. And it went on forever. Which is like a whole WORLD of scary. Anyway, I was about to swallow real loud when Montgomery Kensington tackled me to the ground. So I'm lying there on the ground next to Montgomery Kensington. "There's a troll in the woods with a bow and arrow," he said, "so I wouldn't stand about admiring the view for too long."

"A *troll*? With a bow and arrow? You're kidding me?"

"Would I kid a kidder? Take heart, old fruit. Troll sightings are pretty rare these days. But some blighter has taught this one how to shoot a bow. Some blighter from this very school."

"What kind of a blighter … I *mean,* what kind of an *idiot* would have done that?"

"I haven't the foggiest. But the headmaster is looking into it. And when he finds out who's responsible, well … they'll be sorry they ever gave archery lessons to a troll." Then he waved his finger in my face like I was the very blighter … I mean, the *idiot* who gave the troll archery lessons. Anyway, even though I was lying on the floor, I could see there were two beds and two desks in my dorm. I was about to ask Montgomery Kensington who the other bed and desk were for when he jumped up. "Must dash!" he said, and then he ran out the door. And then the door creaked closed like it was pushed by a ghost. So there I was, Jimmy Drummer, the world's most regular guy, lying on the floor in a school for wizards, surrounded by a forest with a troll in it, and a room that maybe had a ghost in it. For an everyday dude, I knew I was having a pretty rough day. But there was no way I was going to spend the rest of it lying on the floor. So I stood up. And that's when I noticed it: the white chalk outline of a person on the carpet *right* under my feet. And that's when I heard it: someone clearing their throat in the room. So I spun about and blinked towards this fireplace that had two armchairs in front of it. Man, I couldn't believe my eyes. A tiny lighter-shaped bottle was floating in front of the armchairs, right beside a floating pipe. I was already pressed right up against the wall when this kid's voice said, "Has nobody told you how *big* the flies are in these parts? Big as an elf's fist and *twice* as likely to end up stuck in your mouth." So I closed my mouth. And then I opened it again to ask, "WHAT THE HEY, DUDE!" Right then the floating bottle moved towards the floating pipe. And then, no word of a lie, BUBBLES started puffing out of an invisible mouth. You heard me right. Bubbles. So anyway, one of those flies that everyone kept talking about flew in the open window. Man, that thing was like the size of a *kitten*. So I was about to scream, but I figured closing my mouth made more sense. So I was scanning the room for a can of bug spray the size of a fire extinguisher when those bubbles the invisible dude was blowing turned into bubble spiders and chased the fly out the window. So I ran to the window and slammed it shut. Anyway, I'm staring out the window at the scary-as-hell forest, almost too afraid to move, when the voice in the room said, "If I were you I wouldn't stand *there* for too long. The last fellow to admire the view from that window ended up as that chalk mark on the floor." Man, I had to dig deep for some regular dude courage. I must have found some, too, 'cos I turned round and shouted, "Where *are* you, man!?"

"My location is elementary. You see my pipe?" Right then the pipe waved about a little. "And the bubbles?" He must have tilted back his head, 'cos some bubbles streamed up towards the ceiling. "So where do you deduce I must be sitting?"

"*What?*"

"From where in the room is my voice emanating?"

"What? And *what*?" Man, I was saying 'what' so much I thought maybe I was turning

into an English dude. "From the location of the pipe and bubbles, where do you *think* I am?" the voice asked.
"In the chair by the fireplace!"

"You *are* him. The boy with extraordinary powers," said the voice.

"What? No! It was obvious where you were sitting." Right then this kid appeared in the armchair. "Welcome to the Skyforest Wizard School," he said. "I'm Marty Holmes. You may have heard of my great, great, great, great, grandfather Sherlock?" Just when I thought my day couldn't get any weirder, it went and found a whole new level. "You have *got* to be kidding," I said. But I knew it had to be true. You only had to look at this little guy to see that he was a Holmes – a big nose for sniffing out clues, a funny-looking pipe, a red dressing gown with an H sewn into it, a pair of gold slippers … *and* a magnifying glass. So he got up and came over and peered at me through his magnifying glass. He examined me like I was a clue or something. "Extraordinary," he said.

"Do not say that, dude. Don't ever say that. All I ever wanted to be was a regular guy. A beach bum. Maybe a surfer dude or ..." I realised I was starting to babble. So I closed my mouth. That Holmes dude's eye sure looked MASSIVE on the other side of that magnifying glass. "There's really no need to look like a startled rabbit," he told me. "I deduce we have a lot in common."

"You could have fooled me," I said. Then he grabbed hold of my hand and shook it. "I don't want to be a wizard either! I want to be detective."

"No kidding? I could tell that already."

"Extraordinary."

"Not really. A startled rabbit could have deduced that," I told him.

21

"Bravo! I therefore deduce that you are an expert on the subject of startled rabbits," he said, blowing a bubble in the shape of a startled rabbit. If you're wondering what a startled rabbit looks like, it looks just like a regular rabbit, only startled. Anyway, I obviously don't know the first thing about startled rabbits. So I deduced that maybe this Holmes dude was actually pretty lousy when it came to making deductions. "A startled rabbit expert in our very midst. How very extraordinary," he said. It felt like I couldn't win. It really did. And that's when I heard it. This *other* voice in the room. A girl's voice that said, "So the prophecies ... they *are* coming true. You both want to be rid of your magical powers. So you can be like *regular* people."

"You, ah ... you *heard* that too, right?" I asked the little Holmes dude.

"Allow me to introduce my colleague, Mazy Bates," he said.

Right then this girl appeared in the other armchair. And the first thing she said was, "Has nobody ever warned you about the size of the flies around here?" So right then I deduced that my mouth must be wide open. Oh, man ... Mazy Bates. She has the blackest hair and the bluest eyes a regular dude is ever likely to see. I guess what I'm trying to say is ... what I need you to know about this Mazy Bates chick is ... well, there's really no way of saying this without sounding like a total loser but ... she's a total stunner. So I'm thinking this is like the ONE TIME when I wouldn't mind someone thinking I'm extraordinary. So I muttered, "I'm Jimmy Drummer and I'm ..."

"Not in the least bit extraordinary," she tells me.

"There's no time like the present!" said Marty.

"And no time could suck like the present," I muttered.

"I deduce you have an audience with Professor McDougall in precisely 10 minutes!" said Marty.

"Excellent deduction, Holmes," said Mazy.

"It was elementary," said Marty, waving a sheet of paper in my face. "This letter was delivered here by a raven this morning. And it clearly states that the hour of Jimmy's meeting with professor Marcus McDougall is at 10pm today. A glance at my pocket watch informed me that it is now 9.50pm. So I was able to deduce he has 10 minutes to get there."

"I can tell the time too," I told Mazy, pointing out my wrist watch.

"No doubt. Any six-year-old can *tell* the time. It takes a true genius to *deduce* the time," she said. So I'm thinking, what's the difference? There *is* no difference. And then I wondered if Alice felt this freaked out when she fell down that rabbit hole into Wonderland.

One minute later …

So, one minute later I'm walking along this big spooky corridor with Marty and Mazy. "Who is this Professor Marcus McDougall anyway?" I asked them.

"Well, what do *you* already know about him?" asked Marty.

"I don't know anything about him. I only heard about him five minutes ago, dude."

"That's where you're wrong. You know more than you *think* you know. For a start, what do you deduce about the professor from his name?"

"Well, that he's a *professor*?" I said.

"An extraordinary deduction," said Marty, patting my back.

"Oh, yeah, extraoooooordinary," said Mazy, rolling her eyes.

"What else have you deduced about him?" said Marty.

"Well … that he's a *Scottish* dude?"

"Another extraordinary deduction," said Marty.

"Oh yeah, extraoooooordinary," said Mazy, rolling her eyes back the other way.

"And what led you to conclude that he's Scottish?" said Marty.

"Well … Marcus McDougall sounds like a Scottish name, I guess."

"Extraordinary," said Marty, shaking my hand.

"Oh yeah, extraoooooordinary," said Mazy, rolling her eyes back into the middle. I couldn't believe it, I really couldn't. The one person who I couldn't care less what he thought about me thought I was extraordinary. And the one person I wanted to think I was extraordinary thought I was extraoooooordinary. Which is like the total opposite to extraordinary. If this was like a rabbit hole, I wanted out of it. I really did. And that's what I was going to tell this Professor Marcus McDougall dude. So anyway, we're walking through this great hall. It had all these suits of armour in it. Loads of them. About a hundred down each side. Half of them were holding swords, and the other half had these spiked balls on chains. So I was thinking how lucky it was that those suits of armour didn't have any knights inside them. "It means there's no way they can use those weapons on us," I muttered. That's when we heard this 'CLASH!' and turned to see that two suits of armour had come to life. And the one with a ball and chain must've taken a swing at the other one with a sword, 'cos the one with the sword didn't have a helmet … or a head. "Tell me this kind of thing is normal around here," I said.

"It's the first time I've seen it," said Marty, puffing exclamation mark bubbles out of his pipe.

"*You* must have done this," said Mazy, flaring her nostrils at me.

"What? You mean with my extraordinary powers?" I said. Crazy I know, but I couldn't help smiling when I said that.

"No! With your irresponsible babbling!"

"I didn't *babble* a single thing about all these suits of armour coming to life and *fighting*!" I said. I guess that's when *all* the suits of armour came to life and started fighting. You have any idea what 200 suits of armour hitting each other with swords and spiked balls on chains sounds like? Noisy as hell.

"Take your fingers out of your ears and fix this!" said Mazy.

I still wanted to impress her for some reason. And it seemed this was the ideal time to show that maybe I am just a little bit extraordinary. So I took a deep breath and yelled, "Stop with the fighting, iron dudes!" So the iron dudes stopped fighting like I startled them. "Problem solved," I said, feeling pretty good. And that's when all those iron dudes clanked around to face us. All 200 of them. And charged! "I've made an important deduction," said Marty, puffing on his bubble pipe.

"What is it, Marty?" said Mazy.

"That now would be the perfect time to *run*," Right then all the bubbles he puffed turned into little running bubble dudes and took off.

"Run? Yes! Brilliant," said Mazy.

"I could have told you that running was a good idea!" I said.

"Oh, *really*. Well, we wouldn't be in this mess if not for your ..."

"Extraordinary powers?" I said.

"Irresponsible babbling," she said, flaring her nostrils again. I guess that's when she pulled a magic wand out of her blazer. "Ex-mara-mus-freeze-es-armour-present!" she said, doing a figure of eight with her wand. So right then all the suits of armour got frozen in ice. "Cool," I muttered. "The ice won't hold them for long," said Mazy. So we turned and followed the running bubble dudes. And behind us we could hear crashing and splintering noises as those suits of armour smashed out of the ice. Anyway, we were running through this narrow corridor when Mazy said, "Quick! Under here!" Then she dived onto the floor and slid under some benches. So Marty and me did the same. "This is all your fault," she tells me, wriggling her feet right in my face.

"What? I never asked for *any* of this," I said, wriggling my feet in Marty's face.

"I deduce this is not the time to argue. But the time to act as a team," said Marty, wriggling his feet in no one's face. "And I also deduce that we need to come up with a plan to get those hollow knights back where they belong," said Marty, puffing little question marks out his pipe.

"Exactly, brilliant Holmes," said Mazy.

"Huh?" I said, "*Anyone* could have deduced that we needed to *come up* with a plan."

"Oh, *anyone* could have done it, could they? Well, I didn't notice you doing it," she said, wriggling her feet in my face again.

"Well, maybe I don't get off coming up with stuff that's, like, TOTALLY OBVIOUS," I said, wriggling my feet in Marty's face.

"How dare you?" Mazy tells me. I guess that's when she sorta kicked me right on the nose. "Ouch!" I said.

"Have you forgotten my last deduction?" said Marty. "We must work *together*."

"Sorry, Holmes. I propose we get to the library and find the appropriate spell to fix the mess Jimmy's made with his irresponsible thoughts and babbling," said Mazy.

"And what's more, I deduce we need to reach the library without the hollow knights killing us first," added Marty.

"I agree, Holmes," said Mazy. Right then I shook my head like I couldn't believe my ears. It was clear this little Holmes dude *was* the master of something. And that something was deducing THE MIND-NUMBINGLY OBVIOUS. So I reasoned this Mazy chick must like hearing THE MIND-NUMBINGLY OBVIOUS. So I thought maybe I should give it a go. So I said, "You know what, guys?"

"What?" said Marty, and he actually sounded interested.

"Amaze us," said Mazy (and she really didn't).

"Well, it's like this," I said, "there is *no way* we should let those knights stick us with their swords ... And ... it's like, there is NO

WAY we should let them hit us on the head with those spiked balls either." I'm lying there, ready to lap up all the praise when Mazy said, "*Oh my God*. The boy's obviously *simple*." So I'm about to slide out and find Montgomery Kensington and tell him I want out of this crazy rabbit hole. "I ain't no Alice in Wonderland!" I said, sliding out. Then I slid right back in again when I saw a hollow knight come stomping into the corridor. And that's when it occurred to me. "You guys must know some kind of invisibility spell, right?"

"Of course," said Marty. "Invisibility is the perfect solution for reaching the library in three pieces. A brilliant deduction, Jimmy."

"But *he* can't make himself invisible. *He* can't even do the most basic spells," said Mazy.

"So what do you deduce we should do?" Marty asked her.

"Maybe an invisibility huddle?" she said.

"Brilliant!" said Marty.

So, as soon as the coast was clear, we slid out and they huddled around me. Then Mazy waved her wand over our heads. "Ex-dissaperus-hallus-now!" she said. Man, you might think walking down a spooky corridor in an invisible huddle with a couple of wizards sounds cool. Well, think again. You just feel like a pair of eyeballs floating down a corridor. Which is a *seriously* freaky feeling for a regular dude. I guess that's why I started looking left and right for Marty and Mazy. I couldn't see them. They were invisible. But I managed to head-butt them somehow. "Hey! What are you doing *now*?" said Mazy.

"Arrrgh!" said the little Holmes dude, hitting the carpet with a thud. "Quick! Grab Marty!" said Mazy. Which is not as easy as it sounds when you can't see yourself or the person you're supposed to be grabbing. So I reached down for Marty's invisible shoulder ... "What's *this*?" I said. "You magicked up a *bowling ball* or something, dude?" Marty suddenly sounded real nasal, like he caught a cold while he'd been down there. "That's not a bowling ball, Jimmy. I deduce you've stuck two fingers up my nose … possibly three … maybe even four," he said. So that's when I yelled, "GROSS!"

"I *told* you this guy was going to get you into all sorts of trouble, Marty! But even I didn't think he was going to stick four fingers up your nose … right before he got you killed!"

"I didn't stick my fingers up his nose on purpose! What kind of a *freak* do you take me for?" So anyway, we yanked Marty back to his feet and got back into our huddle. "We need to move out of this corridor!" I whispered. So we started to huddle down the corridor away from the clanking. Then we huddled around a corner into another corridor, and heard some knights clanking up behind us. So we huddled against the wall until they clanked past us. Then we huddled up a staircase, and down this other staircase, and across a hall towards these massive red doors. "Open-librus-to-student-passus," whispered Mazy. So the doors started to open outwards. I guess that's when the invisibility spell started to wear off, because I saw flashes of our feet. And that's when this hollow knight spotted us. "I deduce we should run," deduced Marty, puffing some more of those running bubble dudes. So we ran into the library and turned to see the doors slam shut on that knight. "This is the Domed Library," said Marty. "It's called the Domed Library because of that *dome*," he said, pointing up at a dome. This was the kind of 'STOP THE PRESS!' deduction I'd come to expect from Marty. Right then, a hollow knight started to hit the doors with a spiked ball. "To the solution!" said Mazy, running off to this wall of books.

"To the solution," said Marty, walking off towards this other wall of books.

"To the *solution*?" I muttered, staying put.

"Whatever you do, *don't* open that door with your irresponsible babbling," said Mazy. Then she grabbed a big green book and started flicking through its pages.

"I get that. I'm just going to stand right here and keep it zipped," I said. *There's no way I'm going to start babbling about opening those doors,* I thought. So right then the doors started to open. "The doors are opening," said Marty, turning a page of this purple book and puffing the word 'solution' out of his pipe. That's the one thing I have to admit *is* pretty impressive about Marty: he sure is cool under pressure. Unlike Mazy. "What did I just tell you about the door!" she screamed at me.

"I didn't babble a word about it!" I said.

"But you went and *thought* something really stupid, didn't you?"

"Well ... how am I supposed to stop myself *thinking* stupid things! That would be, like ... impossible!" And then I realised what I said and wished I hadn't said it. Anyway, these four knights came clanking right at me. And I'd had enough. I really had. So I grabbed this heavy book off a table and hurled it at them. And then I threw another and another, and I *wished* I could throw *ALL the books!* Then we all froze ... and listened to this rumbling sound. Man, all the books in the library – and I'm talking *thousands* of them – started bouncing around on their shelves like they were coming to the boil. So I looked at Marty and he's puffing these *massive* question marks out of his pipe. And then I looked at Mazy and she's *completely* freaked. Then she said, "Whatever it is you're thinking, Jimmy Drummer ... STOP THINKING IT!" You ever tried to *stop* thinking about something once you've started thinking about it? So I thought: *I STILL wish I could throw every darned book in this darned library at those darned knights!* "DUCK!" said Mazy. So I looked about for some kind of freaky duck. And then noticed that Marty and Mazy were lying on the ground with their hands covering their heads. Man, I hit the deck just as the world seemed to end in an explosion of books that flew through the air like missiles. I'm talking thousands of 'em that buried those knights *completely* and made a mound of books that reached all the way up to the ceiling. The door was totally blocked. "I deduce that you believe it now," Marty said to Mazy. So I looked over at Mazy. She's sitting cross-legged on the floor and gazing around like it's the first time she's ever seen a library. "It's extraordinary," she said. And I guessed she was talking about what I just did. And then she looked at me and said, "I *believe* it."

"That's why I deduced that Jimmy can help us stop Ralph Ratson and his evil cohorts," said Marty, puffing this ugly-as-hell-looking bubble dude.

"Ralph *Ratson*?" I said. So Mazy stood up and crossed her arms like she just felt a chill. "Ralph Ratson is a bad wizard kid. The *worst*. And he's somehow fooled every teacher in school into thinking he's the nicest student that ever came here. But *all* Ralph Ratson wants is to be is the evillest, most powerful wizard that ever lived. Just like his grandfather used to be."

"And the Flippety Jibbit can grant him that power, Jimmy. That's why we have to find it before he does." I guess what they'd been saying up until then sounded like pretty serious stuff. I mean, I didn't like the sound of this Ralph Ratson and his evil cohorts one bit. But all I could think to say was, "Did you just say the *Flippty Jibbot*?"

"Flippety *Jibbit*," said Mazy.

"So what's a Flippety Jibbit?" So Marty started to puff really hard on his bubble pipe. And out of his mouth he blew this bubble cup with four handles. It looked like some kind of freaky trophy. "If the drawings are to be believed ..." puffed Marty, "it looks something like this."

"The Flippety Jibbit has been hidden in the school's deepest dungeon for 300 years," said Mazy, "and you have *no idea* how close Ralph Ratson came to finding a way into that dungeon last term."

"What's so special about this Flippety Jibbit thing anyway?" I asked.

"It has the power to grant three wishes. One of those wishes has already been used ... it built *this* place ... the Skyforest Wizard School," said Mazy.

"But *two* wishes remain," said Marty. "and I deduce that's the *exact* number we need to turn me into a regular detective, and you into a regular dude."

"But more importantly, *somebody* has to use those two wishes before Ralph Ratson does," Mazy said. Boy, did that Flippety Jibbit sound like the ideal solution. Anyway, that's when the mound of books started to rumble … and a Professor Marcus McDougall-shaped gap appeared right in the middle of it. And through this gap walked Professor Marcus McDougall. This professor dude was enormous. Even his red beard looked longer than me. And it only came down his waist. And another thing: this guy's shoulders looked like battering rams. So Professor Marcus McDougall cast this long shadow over me. And that's when I heard myself gulp. And then in a Scottish accent he boomed, "I was expecting the new pupil in my study 10 minutes agoooo."

"We're very sorry, Professor Marcus McDougall," said Mazy, "but we had a spot of bother with some armour."

"Aye. That you did," he said, looking at me. "And there will be noooo more talk of Flippety Jibbits. Do you hear me, Holmes? I should have knoooown you'd volunteered to come back to school early for a reason, lad."

Marty shrugged his shoulders.

"Dinnae shrug your shoulders at me, Holmes. Not unless you want to be shovelling unicorn muck out of the stables for the rest of the week. Now you listen to me, laddie. And you listen good. Noo-one who ever went looking for the Flippety Jibbit was seen nor heard from again! Least of all a wee detective and an American *dood* who doesn't understand the first thing about his powers."

"What about me?" said Mazy.

"What about you? It takes more than a wee lassie with a feisty nature and a rudimentary knowledge of magic to survive the Flippety Jibbit Dungeon."

"But *together* ..." muttered Marty.

"Together you would have got yourselves lost for good! Or worse! Now dinnae test my patience any further, lad." Then he uncurled this long finger and pointed it at me. "You follow me, laddie."

5 minutes later …

Man, Professor Marcus McDougall sure takes long strides. And when he walks, his red and black robe billows up and hits you right in the face. So I slowed up a little as I followed him down corridors and up corridors and downstairs and upstairs and outside into this courtyard and then back into the school and up this winding staircase to his office. He didn't say a word to me the whole time. So I figured maybe he was mad at me for trashing his library. But I didn't care if he was mad. I really didn't. I didn't ask for any of this. Spooky old schools and magic and wizards and wands and exploding libraries and flying cars and trolls with bows and arrows and invisible huddles and ... and, AND! ... Man, I'd worked myself up into quite a state by the time we got to his office. So he sat down behind this desk that had so many books piled up on it I could only see the tip of his pointy hat. Did I mention the dude wears a pointy hat? Well, he does. They're obviously very popular in these parts. "Sit down," he told me. I was so mad there was no way I was going to do what some old hat told me. So I made a point of standing as upright as possible. "Now you're sitting comfortably, we can begin," he said. "And if you're wondering about the mess, I have a wee spring-clean this time every year."

"It's *summer*," I told the hat.

"I'm late this year."

"I don't care. It could be Christmas for all I care. And one more thing ..."

"Yes, laddie?"

"I don't want to be a wizard."

"I don't want tae spring clean in summer, but needs must."

"That's different. I don't *belong* here."

"And where is it you think you belong, laddie?"

"In a regular school with regular kids."

"Out of the question. You're here because you have extraordinary powers. And you must be taught how to control them."

"But I don't want powers! Take them away and give them to someone who does. Like Mazy!"

"That canne be done."

"But aren't you like some powerful wizard?"

"I can noooo more remove your extraordinary powers than change your personality. Enough now! I summoned you here early so you can get used to your surroundings before the new term begins."

"Get *used* to them? How can a regular dude get used this place?"

"Get used to it you will. Now I'll admit they can be a bit of a handful at times, but Marty Holmes and Mazy Bates know the workings of this school inside and out. There's much you can learn from them. At least, when they're not talking about finding dangerous artefacts."

"You mean the Flippty Jibbot?"

"Flippety Jibbit. And that I am, lad. But put such crazy talk out of your mind. That's a path to certain DOOM," he said, standing up and casting that long shadow over me again. Then he paced up and down and told me what was expected of Skyforest Wizard School students. Stuff like 'excellence' and 'diligence' and 'perseverance' and a bunch of other words I didn't even recognise. Then he pulled this cord that was hanging by his desk and told me he'd summoned a hunchback called Dave to escort me back to my dorm. Yeah, you heard me right, a hunchback called Dave.

Five minutes later ...

So, five minutes later I'm walking behind this dude with a hunched back and a massive key chain on his belt. That belt had at least 500 keys hanging from it. Apart from his hunched back, and his right eye being, like, three times the size of his left eye, *and* his feet being the size of mini surfboards, Dave seemed like a pretty regular dude. Like a janitor or something. So I tried to strike up a conversation with him. "How's it going, Dave?" I asked him.

"DAAAVE!" he said, like he's really excited about his name.

"Jimmy!" I said, like I was excited about my name too.

"DAAAAAVE!" he said, like he was even more excited about his name than he was two seconds ago.

"Nice to meet you, dude," I said. "I'm just a regular guy like you. So what's it like being a janitor in this place anyhow?" So Dave pulls this weird face. And if I'm honest, Dave's face was probably weird enough already. "I bet working here is pretty crazy, huh?" I said.

"DAAAVE!" he said again, clapping his hands. I figured conversation probably wasn't Dave's thing. Anyway, we went into this small room and he closed the door behind us. So we're standing nose-to-nose in this little room that has *nothing* in it. No furniture. No pictures. Nothing. And Dave was staring at me with his big eye (I guess the small eye is difficult for Dave to control 'cos it keeps going round and round in circles). "...What, ah ... what are we doing in this little room, dude?" I asked.

"Extra-ordin-ary-eth?" he said, peering at me. At least, I think that's what he said. Dave's tongue is so big it kinda gets in the way of his words. So I said, "There's nothing extraordinary about me. I'm just a regular guy like you. So how long do we have to stand in this little room?"

"*Extra-or-dinary-eth*???" he said, looking me up and down.

"No, man. Like I keep telling you, I'm just a regular guy. So about this little room … is it a dead end? Are you lost?"

"Ext*ra-or-dinary-eth*??????" he said, shaking his head like he couldn't *believe* I was extra-or-dinary-eth.

"Look, man," I said. "I'm not real keen on small rooms. Maybe I got that thing – what do they call it? *Claustrophobia.* I just need to know why we've come in here." So he rolled his eyes and opened the door … onto this *other* floor. We'd been in an elevator. "See!? Like I keep trying to tell everyone. Me most likely to drop out-eth!"

Anyway, I got the feeling the floor he'd taken me to was *down*. Which was a little weird because the dorm I was sharing with Marty was definitely *up*. I mean, this place was dark and cold and looked a lot like a dungeon. So Dave picked up this lamp and lurched down a freaky-looking corridor with bolted doors all the way along it. "You sure this is the right way, dude?" I said. "Professor Marcus McDougall told you to take me back to my dorm. And I don't think my dorm's down here ..." So he stopped at this door and started fiddling with the keys on his belt. "Not thith one, not thith one, not thith one … it's thith one!" he said, and then he opened the door … into the forest.

Less than one second later ...

"Okay. Time out, dude! I *know* my dorm's not out there. But this crazy-as-hell troll sure is!" So Dave pointed a fat thumb right at me and said, "Youeth extra-or-dinary-eth."

"No, dude!"

"Yeth, dud! And I want-eth my bow-eth and arrow-eth back." In case you're having difficulty understanding what he said, he called me a dud and told me he wanted his bow and arrows back.

"Sorry, Dave man, but I can't help you."

"You *not* extra-or-dinary-eth?" he said, narrowing his big eye at me.

"Exactly! Me not-eth extraordinary-eth," I said in Dave-speak. So then Dave mumbled something that sounded like, "Okay-eth, dud," and reached out a hand for me to shake. So I went to shake his hand, and he pulled me past him and shoved me out the door. Man, I spun about to see the door slammed right in my face. I was about to pound on it when a hatch slid up and Dave's face appeared on the other side. "I want-eth my bow-eth and arrow-eth back! You extra-or-dinary-eth dud! So go get-eth my bow-eth and arrow-eth!" And then he slammed the hatch shut. So I gazed up and saw this round tower that seemed to go right up into the sky. And it looked a lot like the tower my dorm's in. So I yelled, "Holmes! Mazy! Heeeeelp me!" Nothing. So the hatch in the door opened again and Dave's smaller eye appeared and started doing loop-the-loops at me. Then the hatch slammed shut right before an arrow thudded into it. So I spun about and all I could see was this wall of trees. And I just *knew* I had to reach those trees to find cover. But that might have meant running *towards* the troll. So anyway, I started running towards the forest. If I'm honest, I wasn't *just* running towards the forest, I was also screaming "THIS CAN'T BE HAPPENING TO A REGULAR DUDE!" as I went. And once I was done screaming that, I heard a thunderclap and this bolt of lightning lit up the sky. And that's when Dave shouted, "GO DUD!" So I looked back over my shoulder and saw the hatch slam shut … right before another arrow hit it. I figured Dave must have some history with the troll. And that's when I *saw* the troll. And this thing wasn't about to win any beauty contests. Man, it was so ugly it made Dave look like a babe. So right then, I *did* do something extraordinary: I ran extraordinarily fast in the opposite direction to the troll. So this arrow whizzed right past my butt. And I was about to dive into the woods when I heard a honk! honk! sound like an old car horn. And that's when Montgomery Kensington pulled his yellow Rolls Royce up alongside me. Man, I was running so fast I was surprised that old thing could keep up. "Splendid night for it, old bean," he said, twirling his moustache.

"For what? Getting shot in the butt by a troll?"

"Hardly, old fruit. I meant for a jog. You are *jogging,* aren't you? And a very impressive jog it is too. More like a sprint, if you ask me."

"This is a sprint, dude!"

"Impressive! Some might even say extraordinary."

"Are you for real?"

"Jeepers!" he said. "You want to have a metaphysical talk while you're out jogging. Am I real for real? Now that *is* an interesting question. And I'm afraid it's going to take a more brilliant mind than mine to answer it. What do you think?"

"I *think* I'm about to get shot in the butt by a troll, dude!"

"Impossible," he said.

"Way possible!" I said, sprinting like hell.

"No. I think you'll find it's quite impossible … because I confiscated that troll's bow not 30 seconds ago."

"You did *what*?" I said, slowing down to a jog.

"I confiscated that troll's bow. You see, I just *happened* to be driving around the grounds when I spotted the troll in question, shooting at something willy-nilly. So! I acted fast. And grabbed the blighter's bow as I whizzed past. That's when I happened upon you having your jog. I see you're slowing down. Need a lift somewhere?"

"You got that right, dude. To my dorm," I said, jumping in the back. So the car took off and I picked up the bow. "Dave the janitor wants this back," I said.

"Oh, he does, does he?"

"He sure does."

"Well, when I explain all to Professor Marcus McDougall, I expect he'll have thing or two to say about that."

1 minute later ...

Montgomery Kensington made his car hover alongside this tall turret. And then he honked his horn. Man, there were so many windows I couldn't tell which was my dorm. But then Marty opened a window and waved his pipe at me. Anyway, I climbed into the front seat and then onto the hood. And Marty reached out and helped me onto the window ledge. After everything, it *almost* felt good to be back in that dorm with the fire crackling and Mazy sitting in front of it. "Thanks for the ride, man," I told Montgomery Kensington.

"Always a pleasure! Never a chore!" he said, taking off.

"Who *is* that Montgomery Kensington dude? I mean, really?" I asked Marty.

"That, my dear fellow, is Montgomery Kensington."

I guess that's the answer I should have expected from Marty. So I asked Mazy. "Who *is* Montgomery Kensington? I mean, really?"

"Montgomery Kensington? He's only the richest wizard in the universe. I'm talking *billions*," she said, rolling her eyes. "He helps out Professor Marcus McDougall sometimes. Nobody really knows why."

"Anyway, enough about MK. You missed quite a show," said Marty, puffing arrow-shaped bubbles out of his pipe. "The troll was running about taking pot-shots at some poor blighter." I wasn't sure what 'some poor blighter' was. But I sure felt like one. "That was me, Marty," I said.

"*You*?" said Mazy. "How did you get outside at this time of night anyway? The whole place is locked up."

"It was that janitor dude, Dave. I guess the troll stole his bow. And because everyone around seems to *think* I'm extraordinary, he thought I could get it back."

"You've only been here a few hours and already you've solved the mystery of the Troll's bow. Extraordinary," said Marty.

"I didn't solve a thing, dude. I just got shoved out a door and ran."

"Anyway, you're back now ... and there's something important you need to see," said Mazy. Boy, did she sound serious. Then she opened a wooden chest under the window and took out an old book. "We borrowed it from the library ... and we'd never have found it if you hadn't turned the place upside down," she said.

"What's in it?" I asked.

"Very important information ... about finding the Flippety Jibbit."

Half a second later …

"Look," I said, "*nobody* wants to be a regular dude as much as I do. But there has got to be some other way. The Prof said that *no one* who ever went looking for the Flippety Jibbit was ever seen or heard from again. Which sounds like *way too long* to go AWOL."

"That's why we *have* to find it," said Marty, puffing smiley faces out of his bubble pipe. Or maybe they were crazy faces. Who could tell? So Mazy crossed her arms and said, "If you'd *ever* read a Sherlock Holmes story, you'd know that Sherlock Holmes liked nothing more than an insurmountable challenge."

"Huh?" I said.

"Oh, sorry. He liked to do things that seemed like they were impossible." There was something I had on my mind. And it's not like I wanted to bring it up. But it seemed like I had no choice. "I hate to be the one to tell you, but … Sherlock Holmes isn't real. He's just a character in a book that someone made up." So Marty and Mazy stared at me so long and so hard I thought maybe Montgomery Kensington had turned them into shop dummies. Then they burst out laughing like I was the world's greatest dummy and I'd just told the world's funniest joke.

"Sorry, Jimmy," said Mazy, "but fictional characters *are* real. That's one of the very first things we're taught in wizard pre-school."

"There's a wizard *pre-school*?" I said.

"Of course," said Marty, drying his eyes and puffing bubble gold stars.

"And one of the *first* things we're taught at wizard pre-school is that there are *two* worlds," said Mazy.

43

"There's the world we live in," said Marty, puffing bubble planet Earths. "And then there's the *Other* World. And that's where the characters from books are," he said, puffing bubbles in the shape of this Other World. I guess this Other World has two moons and a giant pen orbiting it. "And one of the coolest things about being a wizard is we can visit the Other World of fictional characters. But only after we graduate and get our wizard's passport," said Mazy. Then she opened the book and we gazed down at this old drawing of a golden cup with four handles … and right behind it loomed this fierce-looking dragon. Right under the drawing it said: Φλιππετψ γιββιτ.

"What's with the weird words?" I asked.

"It's ancient wizard dialect … for Flippety Jibbit," said Mazy.

"And, ah … what's the deal with the *dragon*?" I asked.

"The Flippety Jibbit is guarded by it," she said.

"Okay. Time out," I said. "That explains why no one who ever went looking for it was seen again. They ended up as dragon chow."

"But don't you *see*?" said Holmes.

"Sure I do. I see *a dragon*, dude."

"But you're forgetting something. Something important," he said.

"Oh, yeah? What's that?"

"Your extraordinary powers. Just *think* about the library."

"You're kidding me, right? That's no library, man. That's a *dragon*. And I'd rather be a crazy wizard than dragon chow any day."

"Well, maybe this will change your mind. We didn't want to show you this. But you've left us no choice," said Mazy.

"Show me what?"

"A glimpse into your future, just one week from now … on the first day of the new term," said Marty. So that's when Mazy went over to the fireplace and magicked up this hologram in the flames. And I saw the not-at-all-regular-dudes that I'd be sharing classes with – tall, pale, skinny guys wearing pointed hats and looking all superior. On the blackboard someone had written, 'I just want to be a regular dud.' That's right, they called me a dud, too. And even though I couldn't hear what they were saying, I could see by the way they were scratching their heads and waving their wands in each others' faces that they couldn't agree what a 'dud' looked like. But they sure looked keen to turn me into *something* when I showed up. So anyway, I watched myself walk into the classroom. Man, as if the shock of that blue pointed hat and red robe I was wearing wasn't enough to give a regular dud – I mean DUDE – indigestion, the sight of these three guys pointing their wands at me and turning me into a fly sure was. Boy, it was so humiliating. Particularly when I still tried to eat the candy bar I'd dropped. Anyway, I figured if squaring up to this dragon was my last shot at being a regular dude, I *had* to take it. "Count me in," I said, as I watched this one guy chase me around the classroom with a fly swatter. You can probably guess the name of the dude who wanted to pulp me … that's right, it was *Ralph Ratson*. Man, that dude's eyes are so dark and so close together he looks like a proper rat.

4 seconds later …

So after Marty shook my hand he went over to the fireplace and pulled down on this candle in a dish. The candle bent forwards and the fireplace turned sideways to reveal a hidden room. It looked like a lab full of magic books and scientific stuff. So Marty went in and picked up these three helmets. I guess they looked like bicycle helmets with wizard writing on them. I was about to ask him what they were for when he tossed them over his shoulder, one by one. Then he picked up a bundle of papers and began flicking through them and tossing them over his shoulder, too. "It's here, Holmes," said Mazy, picking this piece of black paper off the floor. "The spell?" said Marty, taking it from her. So Marty started waving the piece of paper above his head like he was trying to get someone's attention. Then he put his hands on my shoulders and said, "We've been working on this spell ever since we heard you were coming here with your extraordinary powers."

"Oh, yeah? What does it do?" So he took his hands off my shoulders and started pacing up and down his hidden room. To be honest, Marty's hidden room is so small he wasn't so much pacing up and down as around and around in circles. So Mazy and me moved to the other side of the room. "About the spell that we've been working on to help us reach the Flippety Jibbit ..." she said.

"Yeah? What about it?"

"It's a huddling spell."

"A huddling spell?"

"Yes. A bit like the one I conjured up earlier that made everyone invisible."

"Oh, I get it! If we're invisible we can sneak in and get that Flippety Jibbit from right under that dragon's fat nose."

"No, we can't," Mazy said. "As you pointed out, this dragon has a fat nose so he can sniff out any invisible intruders."

"So, what's the point of making ourselves invisible?"

"Did I *say* anything about making ourselves invisible? *This* huddle spell is different."

"Different how?"

"Marty will place a hand on your left shoulder while I place a hand on your right shoulder."

"Sounds real friendly. But what's the point if we're going to die?"

"The *point* is that in our free hands we hold our wands. *This* huddle spell will enable me and Marty to use your extraordinary powers for you."

"So what are you saying? That you'll be using me as, like … a *battery* or something?"

"The world's first human Duracell," said Marty, clicking his heels.

A couple of minutes later …

So a couple of minutes later we're huddling down a long corridor on our way to the Dungeon of the Flippety Jibbit. Just like Mazy said, they both had a hand on my shoulders. And in their free hands they held their magic wands. I figured all I had to do was huddle in the middle and make like a battery. But there was something they hadn't told me: I had to hold this umbrella above my head, opened like it was raining indoors. Boy, did I feel like a dummy walking down that corridor holding an opened umbrella. "Tell me again why I have to hold this dumb umbrella?" I said.

"It's not a *regular* umbrella," Mazy said.

"Tell me about it … it has broomsticks and wands printed on it."

"The broomsticks and wands are immaterial," Marty tells me.

"You wanna say that again in English or something, dude?"

"They're not important," Mazy said.

"Okay."

"We need you to hold the umbrella because this spell is FAR from rudimentary," said Marty.

"English, dude! English!"

"The spell is very complicated," said Mazy. "And the umbrella makes sure it's focused on anyone who's sheltering under it." So anyway, we huddled up to this life-sized painting of a two Wizard School kids, standing with their backs to us outside an elevator. And Mazy reached out and poked the elevator button *on the painting*. Nothing happened. The painting just wobbled a bit. And then she poked it again. Man, if we'd been in some fancy art museum on a school trip she would've been arrested for sure. So we were standing under the umbrella and staring at the painting. The two wizard school pupils in the painting were girls, by the way. Real skinny girls with identical blond pigtails. From the back they looked identical. Like twins. I was starting to get fed up with all this art appreciation stuff. So I said, "You do know this is a *painting* of an elevator, right? Not an actual elevator?"

"That's where you're wrong, Jimmy," Marty said.

'BING!' went the elevator in the painting. So my mouth dropped open as the elevator's doors opened. And the two girls walked in and turned to face us. They had purple wizard's robes on and they were *defo* identical twins. So Mazy and Marty took a step forward, but I just stood there. I didn't want to walk straight into a painting hanging on a wall. Even if it had gone all 3D-looking. "Come *on*, move forward!" said Mazy, her nose pressed up against the painting.

"But ..."

"But what? Anyone would think that walking into a painting is the weirdest thing that's happened to you today." She had a point. It didn't even come close to being the weirdest thing that had happened. So anyway, one of the girls in the painting poked her head out the elevator. "Would you like us to hold it for you?" she asked.

"Thanks! We'll be there in a tick," said Mazy. And that's when they sort of bundled me into the painting. So I'm standing in this lift with Marty and Mazy and a couple of twins. Oh yeah … and like a *dozen* fire extinguishers hanging from hooks all over. "What's with all the fire extinguishers? Is this elevator a fire hazard or something?" I asked.

"You'll see," said Mazy, looking up at the ceiling and rolling her eyes.

"Where would you like to go?" said one of the twins.

"To the Hall of the Hollow Knights, please," said Mazy.

"*What*? Didn't we almost get killed by those hollow knights?" I said.

"I deduce that Mazy has a plan," said Marty, sticking his bubble pipe in his mouth and filling the elevator with tiny bubble knights. Then I realised the twins were staring at me. And it kinda wigged me out. "… I'm Jimmy. I'm new around here," I told them.

"I'm Mabel…" said one of the twins.

"And I'm Martha, Mabel's twin sister. And *we've* been around here forever," she said, sighing.

"So, what? You guys hang out in this elevator all the time?"

"Hang *out*. You talk very strangely," said Martha, squinting sideways at me.

"Martha! Don't be so rude! He talks that way because he's from the United States of America. Yes, we *hang out* in this painting all the time," she sighed.

"But why?"

"Because we were *painted* this way," said Martha, looking at me like I must be seriously dumb.

"So, what, you're not actual people?"

"Oh, we *were* actual once. A long time ago when the great painter Grumble came here," said Mabel.

"You see, he asked for two volunteers …"

"To pose outside this elevator …" said Mabel.

"And Mabel put up her hand. So I did too, because we do *everything* together."

"I did not put up my hand first, Martha! You did!"

"Liar, liar, pants on fire!" said Mabel. Right then I smelled burning. And I knew the deal with those fire extinguishers. So Mazy grabbed a fire extinguisher and extinguished Martha's pants. "The twins are painted sprites," she said, giving Martha's pants one last blast. "And they've been having this same argument for the last 100 years."

"*Painted* sprites?" I said.

"Yes. They're here but at the same time they're *not* here. Understand?" said Marty. I sure didn't understand. "... they're like solid holograms," said Mazy. "And painted sprites are very common in the wizarding world. So I suggest you get used to them." Get *used* to them? How was a regular dude supposed to get used to any of this stuff?

"So where are the *actual* twins right now?" I said.

"Off somewhere being grandmothers to little wizards, I expect," said Mazy.

"Okay. So why are we going back to those hollow knights that wanted to kill us?"

"Isn't it obvious?" said Mazy.

"Not real obvious, no," I said.

"If we're going to survive the Dungeon of the Flippety Jibbit ... then we might need some muscle ... some *tin* muscle." Right then Martha fainted and Mabel caught her. "Oh, dear, no! The very mention of the Dungeon of the Flippety Jibbit has caused my sister to faint with fright! Don't you know that no one who ever entered *that* dungeon was ever seen again?"

"Sure do," I said. "I already got the low down from Professor Marcus McDougall."

"And you're still going?" said Martha, coming round in her sister's arms and gazing at me with big puppy eyes. "You must be so very brave ..." she swooned. So right then Martha dropped her sister onto the floor with a thud. The lift doors opened, and we walked out into the Hall of the Hollow Knights.

The hollow knights were all back in their places. Most of them looked pretty beat up, with dents and missing arms and stuff. So we huddled into the middle of the hall. "We're surrounded by hollow knights ... you *sure* you know what you're doing, guys?" I asked them.

"That's rich coming from you," said Mazy, holding her magic wand straight up towards the ceiling. Then I felt her grip my shoulder ... "Ex-knights-areus-summoned-to-bidding!" she said. So all this electricity shot out of her wand. It hit the ceiling and then zigzagged off and zapped the hollow knights. The knights took two marching steps into the room, saluted us, and froze. Man, it was so quiet you could've heard a pin drop. "To the Dungeon of the Flippety Jibbit!" said Marty. That's when Martha squealed in the lift behind us. Mazy rolled her eyes. "To the Dungeon of the Flippety Jibbit!" she said, squeezing my shoulder and waving her wand. I thought we'd have to huddle all the way there, but *oh no*, Mazy went and tapped right into my extraordinary powers and suddenly we were standing in this smelly dungeon with a MASSIVE door ... behind us.

A moment later ...

I noticed that the massive dungeon door was locked and bolted. "Tell me we're *not* in the Dungeon of the Flippety Jibbet," I said.

"That's *exactly* where we are ... about half a kilometre underground," said Mazy, sounding pretty scared for once.

"And not before time ... isn't it marvellous?" said Marty, puffing smiley bubble faces. Man, I figured that either Marty was the bravest dude on Earth or the dumbest. "I deduce we have to go that way," he said, pointing the only way it was possible to go. It was down this corridor with some old lamps that cast eerie shadows over it. I've played Dungeons and Dragons so I knew the deal with dungeons and dragons. "Why, ah ... why not send the hollow knights down there first? You know, to check for any traps?"

"Agreed," said Mazy, pointing her wand down the corridor. "Hollow-follow-expath-toeth!" So the hollow knights started to march past us, through the candlelight and into the darkness ...

30 seconds later …

So half a minute later we heard this crashing and banging like the hollow knights had fallen into a trash compactor. Then we heard *something* coming back our way. Marty and Mazy grasped my shoulder and pointed their wands into that gloom. Out of it stumbled just two of the hollow knights. "I deduce the rest have cleared the path ahead," said Marty.

"Let's *do* this ..." said Mazy. So we huddled down the corridor. Man, something sticky was dripping from the ceiling. It made our feet squelch as we walked. And I was actually pleased I was carrying that dumb umbrella for once. We came to the end of the lit corridor and looked into the darkness. "I deduce that in order to see, we need to shed some light on the way ahead," said Marty, puffing little bubble torches. "Ex-shed-li-on-pa-ahed!" said Mazy, waving her wand. The whole place lit up in this weird glow. It sure was lucky we sent those hollow knights ahead, 'cos *something* had busted them up real bad. "It looks like a junk yard full of trashed armour," said Mazy. "You hear that?" I said. And I guess we all strained to hear what sounded like snoring. The dungeon was round. It's not like there was anywhere for anything to hide. "I deduce that only a very heavy sleeper could have slept through such a racket," said Marty. So Mazy gulped and gripped my shoulder *real* hard. "You know what they say about dragons," she whispered in my ear.

"Not really, no. I'm just a regular dude. Which means I've never actually had a conversation about real dragons my whole life. Well? What do they say about them?"

"... that *nothing* sleeps more soundly than a dragon."

So Marty made another brilliant deduction. "The snoring … I deduce it's coming from a dragon," he said. Then he pulled the umbrella back and we all looked up … and saw this enormous dragon asleep on a ledge high above us ...

1 second later …

Mazy had me in this headlock to stop me running back down the corridor. And, for a babe, she had some grip. "Okay! Let go! I'm cool!"

"Promise me you aren't going to run," she said.

"I'm not about to go anywhere! It's just how any regular dude would've reacted to seeing his first dragon! But I'm cool now."

"We can't break this huddle. If we do we won't be able to direct your extraordinary powers … and we'll be toast for sure," she said.

"I deduce we shouldn't break this huddle, not even for all the tea in China," said Marty, puffing bubble teapots. So Mazy let go of my neck. "That's some grip you got there," I told her. "You work out or something?"

"Only with my wand," she said, pointing it up at the dragon high above us on that ledge. "I deduce that the Flippety Jibbit is up there close to the dragon," said Marty. It looked like there was no way up. So I was thinking maybe we'd have to abort this crazy mission. Man, I should have learnt by now that I shouldn't get my hopes up. Mazy started waving that wand of hers. "Reveal-cli-sta-flip-jibus!" she said. And this staircase appeared at the bottom of the dungeon. Then it started to wind its way up the circular dungeon like it was being built by ghost builders in a serious hurry. "Where is *that* coming from?" I muttered.

"It was there all along. It's just that we can see it now," said Mazy.

10 seconds later …

So were huddling up the staircase towards that dragon. "I deduce
we need to be as quiet as mice," said Marty, blowing little bubble
mice that scurried away. "It's the dragon's nose I'm worried about,"
said Mazy.

"*Really?*" I said, looking up. "It's those gigantic teeth and claws
that are bothering me."

"I deduce those teeth and claws are the least we have to worry
about. Not when that dragon can breathe fire," said Marty.

"Thanks for the reminder about the fire, dude." Man, the higher we
climbed, the bigger that dragon got. So we reached the top. And
even though the dragon was lying flat, its head was as tall as a
house. And that's when it occurred to me that the only weapon I
had was a dumb umbrella. Then Mazy said, "Whatever you do, DO
NOT break this huddle." I guess she thought I might break the
huddle, 'cos I'd started looking around for cover. "We're going to
have to squeeze past the dragon to get to the Flippety Jibbit," said
Mazy. So we huddled right up to it. And around its side we could
see an altar. And sitting on the altar was this golden cup with four
handles. "I deduce that's it," whispered Marty, "the Flippety
Jibbit." So we huddled past the dragon. And we were almost at the
altar when the dragon's nose started to twitch, and its eyes opened
…

1 second later ...

So one second later Mazy had me in another headlock. And we watched the dragon uncurl itself. "Yikes!" I said.

"You can't run!" said Mazy.

"I know that already! I'm cool!" So Mazy let go of my head.

"I deduce we need to use Jimmy's extraordinary powers to create a shield to deflect the fire that's about to ..."

"Crea-a-shied-maxus-circle!" yelled Mazy. The spell must have worked, 'cos the fire went around us. So we backed up towards the Flippety Jibbit. And then out of, like, *nowhere*, those two surviving knights appeared and shoved Marty and Mazy out of the huddle! And before I knew what was happening, I was in this *other* huddle with a couple of hollow knights. Those iron dudes were grasping my shoulders just like Marty and Mazy. And in their free hands they held magic wands. Man, that dragon must've *known* Marty and Mazy had lost their shield, 'cos it glared at them. That's when Marty said something to Mazy. I couldn't hear what he said, but I figured he'd deduced they should run, 'cos that just what they did. I figured Mazy used some kind of sprint spell, 'cos they took off like they had jet packs on or something. And that's when they disappeared right over the edge and fell down into that dungeon room far, far below. So the hollow knight holding my right shoulder lifted his visor. There was someone inside! And I recognised the dude's leering black eyes right away... it was Ralph Ratson.

In the blink of an eye later …

"What the hey, evil dude!" I said. "You trying to get my friends killed or something!?"

"That was a part of my master plan, yes," said Ralph Ratson. What is it with arch villain types anyhow? It's like they always have to have a master plan. Why can't they just get a wish list like normal people? So Ralph Ratson grabbed the Flippety Jibbit off the altar. "And getting my hands on this little beauty is the culmination of that master plan!"

"Huh?" I said.

"It's what my master plan has been all about," he said, sneering down his nose at me. Right then the dragon turned round and breathed fire at us. But the huddle shield deflected it. So then the dragon took a swipe at us with a clawed foot. But that got deflected too. "Thanks to you, the Flippety Jibbit is mine! All mine!" Ralph Ratson told me. Man, he was hugging that thing so close I thought maybe he was going to propose to it. Then he polished it with his sleeve and said, "And now *nothing* can stop me turning myself into the evillest, most powerful wizard that ever lived!" Marty and Mazy had just leapt over that ridge because of this sneering arch villain dude. And it was some drop. I didn't even want to *think* about what might have happened to them. I was getting mad. I really was. So I told Ralph Ratson, "Maybe there's something you haven't figured into your master plan, evil dude."

"Oh yes? And what's that? A regular *dud* trying to stop me?" That's when the other knight lifted his visor and a pale face with a flat nose started laughing like a hyena. That was the last straw. It really was. "I can't let you use the Flippety Jibbit's wishes, arch villain dude!"

"Oh yes?"

"Yes! Because sometimes a regular dude has just gotta do what regular dude's just gotta do, dude!"

"Oh, shut up. Stop babbling about dudes, you idiot. What can the likes of you do to stop me? You're nothing but a regular *dud*." Right then *nothing* seemed to matter except stopping Ralph Ratson. So I did it. I threw the umbrella up in the air. And that dragon toasted it. I knew I must've broken the protection spell, 'cos Ralph Ratson went all slow-mo and screamed, "Nooooooooooooooooo!" And *that's* when I snatched the Flippety Jibbit out of his hands and took off.

4 seconds later …

So I've got the Flippety Jibbit and I'm running like hell. Earlier, when I first got up here, I noticed a crack in the wall just big enough for a regular dude to slip into. And I slipped right in that crack just in time. Man, if not for my pants, that dragon would've singed my butt for sure. So I squeezed as far down that crack as I could go. And then I looked back and saw a dragon eye staring in at me. That eye sure did narrow. And I knew what that dragon was thinking: *it's time to roast a regular dude with extraordinary powers.* Which meant I had to think fast. I guess my hands must have been sweating, 'cos the Flippety Jibbit slipped through my fingers and landed right on my foot. "*!+!* Flippety Jibbits!" I screamed. "Flippety *Jibbits*?" I muttered. "The Flippety Jibbit!" That's when the penny dropped. "It has two wishes left!" So the dragon pressed its jaws right up against the crack. And it opened those jaws wide enough to swallow a truck. I knew flames were about to come right at me. The next thing I knew I'd screamed, "Make the dragon small, tiny, titchy! The smallest dragon EVER! And that's a wish, by the way!" Those jaws shrank so fast it was like the dragon got popped. And then this puppy-sized dragon ran up to me and spluttered a few sparks. Then it started jumping up at my leg like it wanted to play or something. "Sorry, dragon dude. But you left me no choice." And that's when I heard Mazy scream ...

5 seconds later ...

So I squeezed out the crack, ran to the edge of the ledge, and looked down into the dungeon below. Marty and Mazy looked okay. I figured Mazy must have done some kind of floaty spell when they jumped. But they wouldn't be okay for long. I'd never seen a wand fight. Not a real one anyhow ... and, boy, are they brutal. Marty and Mazy had been pinned down behind this rock by Ralph Ratson and his friend. That armour they had on gave them extra protection. And that rock that Marty and Mazy had taken cover behind was being blasted to bits. I had to think fast. I knew the Flippety Jibbit had one wish left. And I had a choice to make. I could either use it get rid of my extraordinary powers and be a regular dude, *or* ... I could use it to save my friends. I figured that if I wished away my extraordinary powers there would be no way to escape the dungeon. Which would've meant I'd have been a regular dude for like *two* minutes before Ralph Ratson blasted me with his wand. And even though Marty and Mazy were annoying at times, I liked them. Man, it was a total no-brainer. So I did what I guess any regular dude would have done: I used the last wish to help my friends. "Transport Ralph Ratson and his hyena dude friend back to their homes! That's a wish, by the way!" So Ralph Ratson and the hyena dude vanished in a puff of smoke.

A couple of minutes later ...

So a couple of minutes later I'd walked down the winding stairs back into the basement dungeon. Marty and Mazy came running over. "What happened to Ralph Ratson and Angus Dreer?" asked Mazy. Marty stuck his pipe in his mouth. "I deduce Jimmy used the Flippety Jibbit to vaporise them," he said, puffing bubble Ralph Ratsons that popped right away.

"You didn't *actually* vaporise them, did you?" said Mazy.

"No. I didn't. I just wished them back home where they're supposed to be right now."

"Well, if you ask me, they deserved to be vaporised," muttered Mazy. "And what about the dragon?" she asked.

"I deduce Jimmy vaporised the dragon," said Marty, puffing little dragons that popped right away.

"Tell me you vaporised that horrible dragon," said Mazy, putting her hands on her hips.

"Well, ah ... actually, no," I said, as the dragon landed on my shoulder and started licking my face. "You turned it into a pet!" she said.

Man, I just shrugged my shoulders. It felt like the only way for a regular dude to end the craziest adventure ever. "That's both wishes used up," said Mazy, "so you're stuck with your extraordinary powers, I'm afraid."

"And I deduce I'll have to be a *wizard* detective forever," said Marty, sighing.

2 hours later ...

I'm back in my dorm now. And my wrist is aching after I just wrote all that down in this 'Magic Box Diary.' I found the diary in my desk. It's like a regular diary, except you write in the air above it and the words fall into the box and arrange themselves. Yeah, you're right, I guess it's nothing like a regular diary. I wanted to put everything down quick so I didn't forget *any* of it. Anyway, right now Marty is sitting in his armchair over by the lit fireplace. He's smoking his bubble pipe and reading a book called *The Science of Deduction*. And Mazy is sitting right opposite him in the other armchair reading a book called *Fighting Evil with Spells and Sorcery*. They're brushing up on their skills for next semester. Ralph Ratson is going to be mad as hell about the way I used the Flippety Jibbit's wishes. Man, he wanted to use those wishes to be the baddest wizard *ever*. But a regular 'dud' wished him home instead. Marty deduced that the fight against Ralph Ratson and his forces of evil was *really* going to kick off next semester. So it looks like I'm gonna have to stick around and learn how to master my extraordinary powers after all. One more thing: there's a dragon sprawled on the rug in front of the fire. I named him Dragon Dude. He's actually pretty cool for a little fella. And I reckon the bigger he gets the cooler he'll be. I'll let you know how things go next semester in my second diary. So look out for it, dudes. And stay regular!

Diary of a Wizard Kid

2

by

Boyd Brent

I'm back! It's me! Jimmy Drummer the wizard kid. And you guys aren't going to believe what's been happening at Skyforest Wizard School. If you thought my first diary was about as crazy as things could ever get for a regular dude then stick around. No word of a lie, right after I finished my first diary the crazy factor went into OVERDRIVE …

Sunday

The new semester starts tomorrow. And all the wizard kids were due back from summer break this morning. Dudes, we're talking a 3000 wizard-kid no-show! So at 11am, I'm sitting in front of the fireplace in my dorm with Marty my dorm mate. If you read my first diary you'll know that Marty is none other than Marty Holmes, the great, great, great, great grandson of the world's greatest ever detective, Sherlock Holmes. And the little dude looks just like him, too. Right down to the pipe and magnifying glass he examines me with whenever he reckons I just said something extraordinary.

"Did you hear that, Jimmy?" he asked me again.

"Hear what?" I said.

"Hear that," he said, looking around the room at nothing in particular.

"Hear what?" I said.

"Hear that?" he said.

"Listen, Marty dude," I told him. "All I can hear right now is you when you keep asking if I heard that. And this book Professor Markus McDougall asked me to study is tricky enough without you asking me if I 'heard that' every two seconds." The book I'm studying is called *Wand Waving for Dummies*. I don't have my own wand yet. So I've been practising with a magic marker. Man,

Mazy found it hilarious when she snatched back the wand she'd lent me and handed me a magic marker. Maybe I had just turned Marty into a Christmas decoration with her wand. But it's not like I meant to do it. "From now on you'll practise with this magic marker," she told me, placing the little green reindeer called Marty on her palm and raising an eyebrow at it.

"What?" I said. "How dumb am I going to look waving a magic marker around?"

"No dumber than Marty looks right now thanks to your waving an *actual* wand," she said, tapping Marty the reindeer with her wand and turning it back into Marty the detective. The end of his nose was a little redder than usual. But apart from that he looked okay. "And besides, magic markers *are* magic," Mazy told me, clicking her fingers in front of Marty's eyes.

"I deduce that's why they call them magic markers," said Marty, sticking his bubble pipe into his mouth and puffing bubble beaks out of it. Marty does that when he's feeling peckish. And that's the thing about this Marty Holmes dude: he wants to be the world's greatest detective, but all he ever does is deduce the mind-numbingly obvious.

"Really?" I said. "Magic markers are really magic?"

"Actually... no," said Mazy. "Magic Marker is the *brand* name. So the worst thing an irresponsible wizard like you can do is... oh, I don't know, maybe *draw* a disaster instead of actually *causing* one with your extraoooordinary powers." If you read my first diary (and you really ought to have read my first diary first – I got this sequence thing going on here, dudes), you'll know that Mazy is this hot wizard chick. And she's the only person I've met since this whole crazy magic trip started who doesn't think I'm extraordinary because of these extraordinary powers I have. No. Mazy thinks I'm 'extraoooodinary'. Which is like the total opposite of extraordinary.

So anyway, back to this morning, just when I thought things couldn't get any worse, Mazy started looking around the room at nothing in particular like Marty had earlier. "Do you hear that?" she said, just like Marty had. I couldn't take it anymore. I really couldn't.

"I can't take any more. I really can't. So I'm going to practise waving this magic marker in your dorm across the hall. Professor Markus McDougall is giving me a wand waving test later, and…"

"You mean a magic marker waving test," said Mazy, pretending to check her fingernails for dirt.

"Whatever. If I fail it…"

"Your magic marker waving test?" said Mazy, pretending to check the fingernails on her other hand for dirt.

"Whatever. If I fail it, he said I'll have to spend the afternoon teaching Dave his 2x table." In case you've forgotten, Dave is a hunchbacked janitor dude with one little eye and one massive eye who almost got me killed when he shoved me through a door into the woods and told me get his bow and arrows back from a troll.

So anyway, Marty walked over to the window that overlooks the enchanted forest and said, "What you *don't* hear, my dear fellow, is the sound of Skyforest pupils flying through their windows into their dorms (at precisely forty-eight kilometres per hour) and crashing into the wall." I'm thinking what Marty said must sound as crazy to you as it did to me when he said it. "What? And why, dude?"

"Why? Because it's tradition, that's *why*," said Mazy.

"Huh? Flying into a wall at forty-eight kilometres per hour and breaking your head on the first day of term is tradition?"

"Nobody breaks their heads," said Mazy, shaking hers.

Marty started puffing on his bubble pipe furiously, which could only mean one thing: he was about to make an obvious deduction. And if you check the shape of the bubbles he's puffing out of his pipe you can get a heads-up on what it is.

"Listen, Marty, man," I said. "If you're about to say nobody breaks their heads because they wear giant snails on their heads, then don't, okay? Just *don't*. At least, not until I've left the room."

"Those are not giant snails on their heads," he said, puffing more kids with giant snails on their heads. "They, my dear fellow, are wizard kid crash helmets."

"You could have fooled me," I told him.

"Of *course* they're crash helmets," said Mazy. "Flying a broomstick into a wall wearing a giant snail on your head would be stupid."

"Oh, really, Mazy dude? If you weren't from the land of crazy wizard people you'd know that flying a broomstick into a wall at forty-eight kilometres an hour sounds dumb whatever you have on your head."

"Be that as it may. I deduce they should have started crashing hours ago. So where are they?" said Marty.

1 minute later…

So I left Marty and Mazy to ask each other 'Did you hear that?' and then gaze about the room at nothing in particular and went into Mazy's dorm to practise for my magic marker – I mean *wand* – waving test. So I'm trying to do this tricky wand manoeuvre that looks like tracing the outline of an angry bat in the air. But to be honest it looked more like a three-legged ground-hog the way I was doing it. And that's when something *swooshed!* right past my head. It hit the wall behind me and left this freaky glowing green stuff all over it.

"Did you hear that!?" I called out to Mazy and Marty.

"We know just what you mean. We hear nothing either!" Marty shouted back.

"No," I said. "There was this *whooshing* sound and then…"

"You heard the sound of *washing*?" Mazy called out.

"No! *Whooshing*! And now it looks like a giant frog just…"

"You heard a giant frog? Washing itself?" said Mazy.

"Just get over here!"

So the first thing Mazy says when she sees the green slime all over the wall is, "Gross! Did you just *sneeze* on my wall?!"

"Ah, no," I told her. "And in case you hadn't noticed I do actually have a *nose* and not an elephant's trunk on my face."

"I deduce that Jimmy is right. There's too much green stuff on this wall to have come from his nose," said Marty, checking out the green stuff with his magnifying glass. "So which way did it go?" he said, turning the magnifying glass to the floor.

"Which way did what go?" I asked.

"The elephant that did this," he said.

"What elephant?" I said.

"The one attached to the trunk that did this?" he said.

"There was no elephant," I said.

"But you just said…"

"I just said that I don't have a trunk on my face! In what way does that sound like I said I saw an elephant sneeze, dude!?"

"So you're telling me an elephant didn't do this?"

"No, dude. For all I know it could have been an elephant. It's just I didn't see an elephant…" At this point I couldn't take any more. I really couldn't. So I walked out of Mazy's dorm and into the next dorm on the landing. And the first thing I spotted when I walked in there was all this green slime on the wall just like the other dorm. But this slime had a broomstick right in the middle of it, stuck flat against the wall. Man, the way all the weirdness was ratcheting up, I knew it was pointless to start waving my magic marker in the shape of a three-legged ground-hog. Besides, the sight of that broomstick stuck to the wall really wigged me out.

"There you are," said Mazy coming into the dorm. "And… *what the*…?" That's right, Mazy had just spotted the riderless wand stuck to the green stuff. So Marty came in and peered closely at all the fresh goo.

"It's identical to the substance in Mazy's dorm, except…" Wait for it, here comes another of Marty's brilliant deductions: "…there's a broomstick stuck right in the middle of it!" he deduced. Which wasn't even a deduction. It was an observation.

"Really, dude? You could have fooled me. I thought it was a three-legged ground-hog."

"Better leave the detective work to me, Jimmy," he said, sticking his bubble pipe in his mouth and puffing bubble bats out of it.

"What, ah… what's with the bats, dude?"

"As in blind as a…" said Mazy, looking at me.

"There's nothing wrong with my eyesight, dude. It was a joke."

"Whatever you say, Jimmy," said Marty, patting my shoulder like I should get my eyes tested.

So anyway, we checked a bunch of other dorms and they all had the same green slime on a wall. Some with a broomstick. Some without a broomstick.

5 seriously freaky minutes later…

So, five seriously freaky minutes later, we were hurrying down this winding staircase on our way to tell Professor Marcus McDougall that all the kids had been turned into slime.

We reached the bottom of the staircase and had a view right into Professor Marcus McDougall's study. All the books on his desk were dripping with the same green stuff. And the professor was nowhere to be seen.

"The plot thickens," says Marty, puffing thickened plots out of his bubble pipe. If you're wondering what a thickened plot looks like, it looks pretty much like a thinned out plot, only thicker.

"Something is very, very wrong," said Mazy, getting out her wand and moving between Marty and me. Then she put her hand on my shoulder like she was about to direct my extraordinary powers.

"I deduce that the whole of Skyforest Wizard School, students and teachers, has been taken!" said Marty, looking all about the room with his magnifying glass at nothing in particular.

"You think Ralph Ratson had anything to do with it?" said Mazy.

"I see no evidence of Ralph Ratson," said Marty.

Then Mazy started to tap her wand against her palm, like she does when she means business. "We ought to go and check Ralph Ratson's dorm for green splodges on his wall," she said.

"I deduce that if we find *no* splodges, then Ralph Ratson and his roommate Angus Dreer are responsible for turning the entire school into slime," said Marty.

5 minutes later…

Five minutes later we pushed open the door to Ralph Ratson's and Angus Dreer's dorm. Guess what, dudes? The back wall, the one right opposite the window, was as clean as a whistle.

"Something smells fishy," said Marty, flaring his nostrils and giving the wall a once-over with his magnifying glass.

"That would be this kipper," said Mazy, holding up a half-eaten kipper she'd just found on a plate beside Ralph Ratson's bed.

"Evidence! I must examine that kipper!" said Marty, grabbing it and practically sniffing it up his nostrils. He stumbled about a bit and almost passed out. Then he said, "I deduce that this kipper has been here since last term."

Mazy wriggled that perfect little nose of hers and said it was gross. And that's when we felt two swooshes, and turned to see Ralph Ratson and Angus Greer turned into slime on the back wall, their broomsticks stuck right in the middle of them.

"I deduce that they must have been running late," said Marty.

"And now they're running down a wall," I said.

"So, if Ralph Ratson isn't behind all this… then who?" said Mazy.

"Or more to the point… *what* is behind this?" said Marty.

"You mean there could be a *what* behind all this?" I said.

"Why not a *what*?" he said.

That's when we heard this rumbling sound and the whole school started to rock back and forth like it was on casters. "Whoa!" I said, as Marty, Mazy and me stumbled down to one end of Ralph Ratson's dorm. "What the…?" I said, as we stumbled back towards

73

the wall with slime on it. "Do something, wizard dudes, or else…!"

So Mazy screamed, "Gross!" and Marty deduced that we were about to "Hit the wall with the slime!"

About a second later…

"What's the point, dudes? I mean, really!" I said as I struggled in the slime.

"What's the point of what?" said Mazy, as she struggled in the slime too.

"What's the point of being wizards if you can't even stop yourself getting stuck in Ralph Ratson slime?"

"How were we supposed to know the school was about to go all 'fun house'?" said Mazy.

So anyway, the school stopped moving and went back to 'normal'.

"I deduce that the school has stopped moving," said Marty.

"Yeah. But now we're stuck in slime..." I said. That's when it occurred to me that we'd been trapped in slime for a reason. And that that '*what*' thing Marty had mentioned may be on its way to do whatever things that people call 'what' do to people.

"Do you… do you hear that?" said Mazy.

No doubt about it: something big was clomping down the corridor. Or maybe that should be stomping *up* the corridor. It's difficult to tell if something is stomping or clomping when you're stuck to a wall in slime.

"I deduce that *something* is coming to get us," said Marty, puffing *something* bubbles out of his pipe. If you're wondering what *something* bubbles look like, use your imagination, dudes. I couldn't bring myself to look.

"You need to magic us out of this slime, quick!" I told them.

"I can't! I dropped my wand when the school started going all sideways and back again!" said Mazy.

So I turned to look at Marty. "Don't *you* have a wand, dude?"

"I prefer to use the art of deduction," he said.

"A fat lot of use your deduction is to us right now," I said.

"That's where you're wrong," he said. "I deduce that we're in big trouble."

I sure was relieved when Marty's deduction turned out to be wrong. Dave burst into the room and yelled, "Two times two equals 128!"

2 very irritating minutes later...

"No, Dave, dude! Two times two is four! Now just get us out of here, will you?" I said.

"Four?" said Dave, scratching his head.

"Yes, it's four!" cried Mazy.

"Foooour?" said Dave scratching his head again.

"Ah ha!" said Marty. "I deduce that two times two is three million and twelve!"

"*What*?" I said. But for some reason it made perfect sense to Dave. And he dragged us out of the slime.

"How did you know Dave would go for three million and twelve?" said Mazy.

"It was elementary," said Marty. I guess when Sherlock Holmes used to say 'it's elementary', he meant it was obvious to him. And only him. So enough with the questions already.

"We need to find out what's happened to everyone," said Mazy, picking up her wand.

"I should think that was bally well obvious," said the happiest, dumbest-sounding English voice you never heard in your whole life. Those of you who read my first diary (and remember I got a diary sequence thing going on here, dudes) will know that that voice belonged to none other than Montgomery Kensington. Just in case you aren't sequenced up, Montgomery Kensington was the dude who came to my mall in Florida where I lived and froze everyone and told me all about my extraordinary powers. He also happens to be the richest wizard that ever lived. So, anyway, we all turned round and saw Montgomery Kensington twirling his handlebar moustache in the doorway.

"It's real good to see you, dude!" I told him.

"And you too, young Drummer."

Mazy put her fists on her hips and struck a superhero pose even though she isn't one. She looked at Montgomery Kensington and said, "It's bally well obvious where they've gone, is it?"

"I should bally well say so," said Montgomery Kensington.

"Well, we're all ears," said Mazy.

So Montgomery Kensington hopped over to the window. No, there's nothing wrong with his legs (relax, he only has two); he just likes to hop. He holds the British hopping record. "This whole business is as freaky as a three-eared rabbit eating cheesecake. With doorknobs on," he said.

"With doorknobs on!" cried Dave.

"That's right, old man," said Montgomery Kensington.

"WITH DOORKNOBS ON!" Dave cried again.

"Yes. That's right. With doorknobs all over, if you ask me," said Montgomery Kensington.

"With doorknobs all over it!" Dave cried again, like there was *no way* he could cope with the idea of so many doorknobs.

"That's right. In fact, it could be said there are more doorknobs on this situation than you'd find in WHOLE MONTH of Sundays."

"MORE DOORKNOBS ON THIS SITUATION THAN IN A WHOLE MONTH OF SUNDAYS!" said Dave. Boy, did Dave look scared.

"Okay, would you please stop talking about doorknobs! You're upsetting Dave!" said Mazy.

So Marty starts to puff bubble doorknobs out of his pipe. "I deduce that Dave has a fear of doorknobs," said Marty, filling the room with bubble doorknobs. I guess all those floaty bubble knobs were the last straw for Dave. He shrieked something about "two times two" being "227 doorknobs!" and ran off down the spooky corridor. Montgomery Kensington started to hop in circles around the room and we all stared at him. "The entire school, teachers and students, has been kidnapped! They're being held for ransom," he said as he hopped.

"Okay. But could you stop hopping for five seconds, dude?" I said.

"He always hops about when he's nervous," said Mazy. "And... *what* did you just say?"

"I just asked Montgomery Kensington if he could stop hopping for five..."

"No! Not you, dufus! I was talking to Monty!"

So Montgomery Kensington started to hop really high like he had something incredibly important to say. "The whole school, students and teachers, has been kidnapped!"

"How do you know that?"

"Because, dear girl, I received this ransom note this very morning," he said, pulling a piece of paper from his pocket and waving it as he hopped.

"I deduce that that note is important evidence!" said Marty. "I furthermore deduce that it might contain important clues as to who has taken them," he said, hopping around the room after Montgomery Kensington.

"It does!" hopped Montgomery Kensington.

So Mazy waved her wand and the ransom note flew out of Montgomery Kensington's hand and into hers. "Oh. My. God," she said, looking at the note and going all goggle-eyed. So I made a deduction of my own: anything that could make a crazy wizard kid go all goggle-eyed was not something a regular dude should hear. Ever. "Take your fingers out of your ears. You really need to hear this," Mazy told me. The fact that I could hear what she'd just told me also told me it was useless keeping my fingers in my ears. So I took them out. "You aren't going to *believe* what's happened to everyone…"

"What's the point of telling us then?" I said.

"They're being held hostage in the Land of Fictional Characters!"

"The Land of Fictional Characters? Doesn't sound so bad," I said.

"Oh, it's bad all right. You ever heard of the Brothers Grimm?" said Mazy.

"The Brothers *Grimm*? No," I said. "But I'm thinking they aren't party dudes. The clue being in the name… Grimm." So I looked over at Marty and saw that he'd turned whiter than the ransom note. Boy, did the end of his nose look red now.

Mazy took a deep breath. "The world that the Brothers Grimm created was amongst the most terrifying fictional places in children's fiction," she said, going even paler than Marty.

"If it was written for children, how terrifying can it be?" I said.

"Think again. The characters those Grimm Brothers created were the stuff of nightmares," said Mazy.

"And?" I said.

"And," she said, "we're going to have to journey to the heart of those nightmares if we're going to save the day."

1 second later…

So, one second later, Mazy had me in this headlock by the door. "No! You can't go 'take a nap!' We're going to need your help!" she said.

"I was going to help! Right after I've had a nap! I'm not like you! I'm just a regular dude! And regular dudes need naps before they travel to nightmarish worlds to rescue wizards!"

"I deduce that we're going to need your extraordinary powers," said Marty, like this was news to everyone.

"I know that! Don't you think I know that!? Okay! No nap! Just let me out of this headlock!" So Mazy let go of my head.

"The Frog Prince!" said Montgomery Kensington, so suddenly that anyone would think the Frog Prince had just walked into the room. I guess that's why we all turned and looked at the door. Nothing but an empty rectangle.

"*What* did you just say?" I asked Montgomery Kensington, rubbing my neck.

"The Frog Prince is the very blighter who sent the note."

Mazy closed the door and went and sat in her armchair in front of the fire. "Even someone like you, who probably never read a book, must have heard of the Frog Prince," she said.

"Sure I've heard of him. My granny used to read the story to me when I was like two. That dude doesn't sound scary."

"What do you know about him?" said Mazy.

"Well," I said, feeling pretty clever for once. "The Frog Prince dude got hexed by some mean old witch and turned into a frog."

"And then?" said Mazy.

"And then," I said, holding my head just about as high as I could, "he gets fished out of a well by this princess, who kisses him and turns him back into a prince. End of story."

"Ah, not quite the end of the story," said Montgomery Kensington. "You see, old fruit, in the *real world* of fictional characters, stories don't end just because the book does. Oh, no. They go on forever and now we're…"

"About to become a part of the story," said Mazy.

"Perfect," I told them. "Just the thing an average dude wants to happen to him: ending up in a fairytale." I shook my head. "I thought this Frog Prince dude was a pretty nice guy. Like a hero. And wasn't he seriously rich? I'm thinking the princess would never have married him otherwise. So what's with the ransom?" That's when Mazy got up and thumped me. "You want to tell me what that was for?"

"For being a chauvinist." I guess a chauvinist is a guy who thinks princesses only get together with princes if they're loaded.

Anyway, Montgomery Kensington got his wand out and magicked up a book. It was entitled *The Ongoing Story of the Frog Prince*. Then he magicked up an armchair. He sat in it and told us to "Gather around now, children. Montgomery Kensington is going to tell you a story."

"Are you joking or something, dude? We're not four years old."

"So you aren't, so you aren't. Well, then, come anyway! And gather round, you warriors in the war against fictional blackguards. And let General Monty bring you up to date." So we moved closer. "Now," he said, "as you know, after the Frog Prince was kissed and turned back into a real prince, he fell in love with the princess who planted the smacker on his frog lips. And without further ado, the prince proposed to the princess, who said, 'Yes!'. She must have thought the prince pretty darned handsome, particularly when compared to the ugly toad he used to be. In the book, they live happily ever after."

"We already knew all that, dude." I told him.

"But this isn't the book," said Mazy.

"Would someone just tell me what could have happened to turn a hero prince into a guy who kidnapped an entire school?"

"By all accounts, the princess had darned expensive tastes," said Montgomery Kensington. "And she demanded the prince buy her this castle and that castle. This palace and that palace. These jewels and those jewels. This carriage and that carriage. Those…"

"Time out, dude!" I told him. "We get it. The princess liked the prince to buy her stuff. So?"

"So everything, old bean. That must be how the prince ran out of money. And, upon hearing about mine, he must have decided to kidnap all the students to blackmail me."

"So just pay the dude," I told him.

"Give in to blackmail? That's not the done thing, old fruit. Not a brass farthing will the prince get."

"I deduce that that can only mean one thing," said Marty, blowing bubble brass farthings out of his pipe. If you're wondering what a bubble brass farthing looks like, it looks kinda like a nickel, only made of brass.

"I deduce that it can only mean one thing," said Marty again. "That we're going to have to travel to the prince's castle, located in the Grimm region of the Land of Fictional Characters, and save the entire school."

"You mean it's down to us to save everyone, including Ralph Ratson," I said, eyeing the closed door.

"Don't even think about it," said Mazy, cracking her knuckles.

5 minutes later…

Five minutes later, I'm standing outside the front of the school with Marty and Mazy. They've got a tandem broomstick they took from a broomstick cupboard. It was built for two and extra long. But there were *three* of us, all bunched up on it. "Talk about a tight squeeze," I said. "You guys would have more room if I got off."

"Stay put," said Mazy.

"You really think my extraordinary powers are up to this?"

"I deduce that we're about to find that out," said Marty, as the broomstick rose straight up into the air. And when I say 'straight up', I'm not exaggerating, dudes. My stomach stayed right there on the ground. Mazy was sitting up front and Marty was behind her, and I was behind Marty at the back. Mazy darted away from the school. I imagined she knew the way to the Land of Fictional Characters. But then she turned about to face the school.

"What are you doing?" I yelled to her. I had to yell because the wind was blowing so hard up there.

"What do you *think* I'm doing?" she yelled back.

"But we just came from that direction," I yelled.

"You want to explain, Marty?" she yelled, pulling the front of the broomstick higher like she was about to do a wheelie.

"I deduce that Mazy is about to fly through the window of our dorm and hit the back wall at precisely forty-eight kilometres per hour."

"She's about to do what?!"

"How else are we going to find the exact spot where everyone's been taken?" yelled Mazy.

"But, but, but, but…" I said.

"But nothing!"

"But, but, but, but… what about our helmets?"

"Tell him, Marty!"

"I deduce that we won't need helmets," Marty said over his shoulder.

"Huh, dude?!"

"I further deduce that we won't actually hit the wall."

"That's right!" yelled Mazy. "We're obviously going to be flying straight through it!"

"And if we don't?" I said.

"Then I deduce we will hit it," said Marty.

Forty-eight kilometres per hour might not sound all that fast to you dudes. Especially when you're flying through the air. But it sure seems fast when you're flying through an open window towards a wall, and…!

A thumping heartbeat later…

I opened my eyes and looked at the bars of the dungeon I was in. I couldn't move my arms because they were shackled to the wall above me. And I couldn't move my feet because they were shackled to the wall below me.

"I deduce that screaming will be quite useless," said this voice to my right. So I glanced to my right and could just about make out Marty's pipe in the darkness.

"What? And flying at a wall and ending up chained to some *other* wall is useful?" I said.

"Just be thankful we didn't hit the wall. It's not like we're dressed appropriately for impact," said this voice to my left. So I looked over my left shoulder to see Mazy chained to the wall.

"Thankful?" I said. "Thankful that I'm chained to a wall in a dungeon?"

"Tut, tut. You really ought to count your blessings more, Jimmy Drummer," said Mazy.

"Let me see… no, I can't seem to think of a single one!"

"I deduce that you're forgetting an important one," said Marty.

"Oh, yeah, dude? What's that?"

"Your extraooordinary powers," said Mazy.

"If I didn't have extraordinary powers I wouldn't even be here right now. I'd be watching a football game or maybe catching some surf or…"

"*Must* you babble?" said Mazy. "This could well end up being the greatest adventure of your life."

"If being chained to a dungeon wall is the greatest adventure of my life, then what's the point? I mean really? What's the…"

"You're babbling again. And babbling is something that's hardly fitting for someone who's destined to use his extraoooordinary powers to become a great wizard."

"A great wizard who's chained to a dungeon wall, you mean?"

"Never fear. I deduce that Mazy has a plan to get us out of these chains," said Marty.

"Oh, yeah? And what makes you say that, dude?"

"Because she wouldn't be so calm otherwise. Isn't that right, Mazy?" he said.

"Well… I might have come up with a plan by now if someone would stop complaining and let me think."

"There you have it, Marty dude. No plan. So it looks like we'll be hanging here unhappily ever after. Perfect. Just perfect. And…"

"Put a sock in it and let me think, will you!" said Mazy.

Right then I tried to come back with a pithy one-liner, but I couldn't because I had a sock in my mouth.

"Extraordinary," said Marty. So I looked at Marty.

"Is there a *sock* in his mouth?" said Mazy. So I swung my head the other way and looked at Mazy.

"It looks like a sock to me," said Marty. So I swung my head the other way and looked at Marty.

"It *is* a sock. A striped one. Stuffed right in his mouth," said Mazy. So I swung my head the other way and looked at Mazy. All this head-swinging was making me kinda dizzy. So I stared in front and tried to spit the sock out. It wouldn't budge.

"Maybe being chained to the same wall as Jimmy means I can access his extraooooordinary powers," said Mazy.

"I deduce that you should test that theory," said Marty.

So Mazy looks at me and says, "Put a potato in it, Drummer!"

"Oh, brilliant. Just brilliant," is what I *would* have said, if that potato hadn't been stuffed in my mouth.

"Release us from these chains!" said Mazy. That's when we all fell off the wall and landed in a heap on the floor. "Quick! Get up! Get up and assume the position!" she said, yanking her wand out of her back pocket.

I took the potato out of my mouth. "What position?" I said.

"I deduce that Mazy means the huddle. The one where we place a hand on each of your shoulders and hold our wands in our other hand," said Marty.

So we assumed the position. "What now?" I said.

"Now we zap the lock on the cell door," said Mazy, zapping the lock on the cell door.

A minute later …

We were in our huddle and making our way down this dungeon corridor that had locked cells on either side.

"I expect all the wizard kids are hung up inside these cells," whispered Mazy.

"Didn't we come to this crazy place to let them out? Shouldn't we be opening these doors, dudes? I mean, the quicker these doors are opened, the quicker we can get out of here," I said.

"There must be over a thousand cells in this dungeon. The last thing we need right now is a wizard kid rabble following us everywhere," said Mazy.

"I deduce that our huddle would soon be too big to fit in this dungeon," said Marty.

"So where are we headed?"

"To find out exactly who's responsible for all this," said Mazy, gripping my shoulder real tight. "I thought we already knew that. The Frog Prince."

"We won't know for sure until we've found him and asked him in *person*."

So I grabbed Mazy and put her in a headlock. "I don't think tracking this dude down is a good idea," I told her. She didn't answer – just waved her wand and *I* was the one in a headlock. "You just used magic!" I spluttered. "That's cheating!"

"Whatever it takes," she said, tapping her wand against my head. And then she said, "Something smells fishy."

"You don't smell so fresh yourself," I said, even though she smelled pretty fragrant.

"I'm not talking *literally*. I mean fishy as in something about this whole situation doesn't add up."

"You want to let go of my head and tell me about it?"

So she let go of my head and told me about it. "The Frog Prince," she said, "was written as a *good* guy. And I don't care what Montgomery Kensington says, when fairytale characters are written as good guys, they stay good. And when they're written as *bad,* they stay really, really, really, really, really BAD. And it's obvious that only a fairytale monster could have done this."

"And I deduce that we must find out who," said Marty.

5 minutes later…

So five minutes later, we're huddling up a creepy staircase that had flaming torches all the way up it. When we finally reached the top, Mazy pushed open this door a little. We all huddled close and looked through the crack. I guess we must have huddled a little too far, because we took a tumble through the door onto the swanky carpet on the other side.

"Quick! Get up! Get off of me!" said Mazy.

So we climbed off Mazy and got back in our huddle. "This is the swankiest, widest corridor I've ever seen," I said, checking out the swanky corridor. Man, that corridor went on for as far as the eye could see in both directions.

"It's a fairytale palace," said Mazy. "What did you expect to find up here? A broom cupboard?"

"I deduce that the prince's quarters are that way," said Marty, pointing all the way down one end of the corridor. Both Mazy and me looked at Marty. It's not like he ever deduced stuff that wasn't totally obvious.

"What made you come up with that deduction, dude?" I asked him.

"It was elementary," he said.

"No it wasn't, dude. Not really. And this looks like the longest corridor in the universe. So I'm thinking, I need to know why I'm going be spending the rest of my life walking to one end of it."

Marty shrugged his shoulders and pointed to a sign on the wall between two swanky paintings. *The Prince's Royal Apartments are that way,* the sign said. "As I said, it was elementary," said Marty.

20 minutes later…

Twenty minutes later, we were still huddling down the swanky corridor.

"It sure is quiet. Shouldn't there at least be servants or something?" I said.

"I know. Like I keep trying to tell you: something smells fishy," said Mazy.

And that's when we reached them. The massive red doors. And when I say massive, I mean MASSIVE, dudes. It was like they had a giant living on the other side of them.

So after some serious heaving, the doors *finally* began to creak open. And right there at the head of this loooooong table with at least a hundred chairs down either side sat this dude dressed in purple like he was a fairytale prince. I must have muttered that aloud, because Marty said, "That *is* a fairytale prince. And I deduce that he used to be a frog."

Man, for a fairytale prince, that dude sure looked miserable. His crown was all lopsided. And so was his face. "What's with his lopsided face?" I whispered to Mazy.

"It's called *a frown*," Mazy whispered back.

I guess that's when the prince beckoned us over with a couple of flicks of his wrist like he was expecting us. "Approach," he said. "You got my ransom note, then? Terrible business. I had to send it. Needed help, you see." Man, he looked so miserable I thought he was going to burst into tears.

"The Frog Prince?" Mazy asked him.

"Woe is me!" he said.

"Woe is you, Your Majesty?" said Mazy.

"That's right," said the prince. "Enough woe to float a woo."

"What?" said Mazy. "Do you know my entire school is chained up in the dungeon of your castle?" The prince looked pretty mad. "Sorry, Your Majesty," she added, curtseying. Then she dug me in the ribs.

"There's no way I'm going to curtsey to this dude," I told her.

"Bow, you idiot," said Mazy. So me and Marty took a bow like we just finished a performance. "That's better," said the prince. Then he blew his nose. "All is quite lost," he said, tossing the

hanky over his royal shoulder.

"Look, dude… I mean, Your Majesty. We're here to help."

"You three? I expected the world of wizards to send an entire army to rescue their young. What can you three do?"

"We can sort this mess out," said Mazy.

"Three children? Against the might of the Mirror Queen?"

Oh, man. When the prince mentioned the 'Mirror Queen', Mazy turned pale and started babbling about her childhood. Then she stuck her thumb in her mouth and started sucking. That's when Marty deduced that 'drastic action' was required.

So I grabbed Mazy's shoulders and shook her until she spat out her thumb. "What the hey?" I asked her. "The Mirror Queen doesn't sound so bad."

2 seconds later…

Two seconds later, I had Mazy in this headlock to stop her running away. "You aren't going anywhere. So are you going to chill, or what? Like I said, the Mirror Queen doesn't sound so bad. And besides, aren't you overlooking something?"

"Oh, what? Your extraoooordinary powers!" she said.

"No. My extraordinary powers. And besides, you're really starting to wig me out. And if we're both wigged out we'll have to put each other in a headlock at the same time. And I'm not sure that's even possible."

So Mazy agreed and I let her out of the headlock.

"The Mirror Queen's reputation precedes her, I see," said the prince.

"Are you *kidding*?" said Mazy. "No one from any story ever scared me more than the Mirror Queen when I was little. That woman is a *monster*." She sat down in a chair beside the prince. I sat down next to her.

"And powerful," said the prince, resting his chin in his palms. Right about then, his face looked more lopsided than ever. "But maybe… *maybe* if you have extraordinary powers, you might defeat her. She's holding my love, my princess captive in her haunted tower."

"Haunted tower?" I said. "Look. You're a prince. In a fairytale. Don't you have an army of knights?"

"I had the finest army of knights ever assembled in this kingdom or any other."

"Had? You lost them?"

"Lost them? Oh, no. They were defeated by *her*."

"I deduce that he's talking about the Mirror Queen," said Marty, blowing busted bubble knights out of his pipe.

"Okay. So maybe we do need to high-tail it out of here. Get some help or something. Because there's no way my extraooordinary powers are more powerful than an army of fairytale knights." I stood up. "So you want to point us in the direction of the real world or something, dude?" I asked the prince.

Right then, Mazy grabbed my arm and pulled me back into my seat. "He's actually a lot braver than he looks," she said, smiling at the prince.

"And a *lot* more extraordinary, I hope," said the prince, sighing.

"So what does the Mirror Queen want with so many wizards? Please tell me it's not what she usually wants," said Mazy.

Marty chipped in. "Having read the story, I deduce that the Mirror Queen must want all their…"

"She can't want *all* their…! That would just be *too* horrible," said Mazy.

"What are you talking about, dudes!? What does she normally want?"

The prince said, "No. She doesn't want to take all their… not *this* time. She wants wizards so she can drain them of their magic. Wizard magic is what she needs to keep her looking young and beautiful now."

"Their *magic*," said Mazy. "What happens to them after she's taken their magic?"

"Who can say?" said the prince.

"So what did she used to take from people to keep herself looking young?" I asked.

Mazy said she didn't even want to think about that. And that if I wanted to find out I should read the story the Brothers Grimm wrote about her.

"So how do we stop this crazy Mirror Queen?" I asked.

"I deduce that we shall need the element of surprise," said Marty, blowing jack-in-the-boxes out of his bubble pipe.

Mazy started to thump her wand into her palm like she does when she means business. "Marty's right! We have to use the element of surprise. It's the only way to defeat the Mirror Queen."

The prince's head dropped even lower. "She sent for the first wizard for draining this very morning," he said. "I was about to go down to the dungeon to pick one when you three arrived. Picking a wizard for draining is a dreadful business for a prince. But if it's the only way to save the princess, what choice do I have?"

"You do have a choice now," said Mazy.

"Oh, yes? And what choice is that?" asked the prince.

"You can send us," she palm-thumped with her wand.

"Oh, goodness gracious," said the prince, shaking his head. "I might as well ask the three little pigs for help. For I fear the Mirror Queen will huff and puff and blow your magic down."

"Less of the three little pigs, dude," I told the prince.

Man, the prince's head dropped so low that his chin was practically touching the table. "And anyway," he moaned. "If she's delivered *three* wizards instead of the one wizard she will smell a rat. And when the Mirror Queen smells a rat, she stops at nothing until the rat is vaporised."

"I guess news of my extraordinary powers has been slow to reach the World of Fictional Characters," I said, sitting up as straight as the prince was slumped.

"That would be because the Mirror Queen kidnapped all the postmen in my realm," said the prince.

"Marty! Those bubbles jack-in-the-boxes you were blowing?" said Mazy, palm-thumping even harder.

"What of them?" said Marty.

"They're the answer to getting us into the Mirror Queen's tower!"

"Ah, ha! I deduce that we're to be the jack," said Marty, blowing more bubble jack-in-the-boxes. But this time, it wasn't a jack that jumped out of the box, it was a bubble version of me, Marty and Mazy.

Right then the prince jumped to his feet and bellowed, "Prepare the box for these three little pigs! I mean jacks!" We were all standing there waiting for a bunch of servants to appear and start preparing the box. But no one showed. The prince slumped back down into his chair. "Oh, I forgot. The Mirror Queen had me send all my servants over to her haunted tower."

"Ex-surprise-us-box for three pigs! I mean wizard kids!" said Mazy, waving her wand in a reverse figure of eight. This big gold box appeared on the table. And right away the lid sprang open and we all jumped back. But nothing jumped out.

5 minutes later…

Five minutes later we were standing outside the castle next to a horse and cart. The horse was called Stewie. I only know the horse was called Stewie because it was a talking horse and it told me. Then it said, "You might want to close your mouth. The fairytale flies in these parts are as big as toads and twice as likely to get stuck in your throat."

"Sorry for gaping, horse dude. I mean, Stewie."

So we climbed up on the back of the cart and sat on the box. "You need to get inside the box," said Stewie over his shoulder. "As soon as we reach the Mirror Queen's forest, she'll send her ravens to spy on us."

"How far is the forest?" I asked Stewie.

"Just yonder past those hills," he said. Marty, Mazy and me got inside the jack-in-the-box. It was a pretty tight squeeze. We had to pull our knees up to our chins.

"I deduce that we're going to need a plan," said Marty.

I couldn't see him. But the bubbles he was blowing kept popping on my face. "We're in a small box, dude. You want to stop blowing bubbles in my face?"

"Blowing bubbles helps him to think," said Mazy.

"Well, you'd better think quick, dudes. I don't think the Queen's haunted tower is far."

"I suppose I'll just have to tap into your extraordinary powers and zap her before she zaps us," said Mazy.

"That's right," said Marty. "I deduce that we'll have to burst out of

98

the box in a huddle and zap her… or something."

"That's *it*?" I said. "We burst out of a box and *zap* her or something?"

"You have a better plan?" said Mazy,

"I thought you were terrified of this witch, or whatever she is? What if you freak out and freeze?"

"I'd rather not think about that. And anyway, we have the element of surprise. I have the spell ready. With your help it will freeze her solid… turn her into a statue."

"You talking permanently?"

"Permanently? What? Ah, *no*. I'm not going to *kill* her. We just need enough time to rescue the princess and get all the wizard kids back to Skyforest."

Stewie had been trotting through the woods for some time. I have to tell you, being a jack inside a box isn't easy, particularly when you're bouncing up and down and being knocked against the other jacks. Man, I never thought I'd be so pleased to arrive at a haunted tower in the middle of a creepy forest. But then I took a peek outside the box and saw the tower. I don't think I ever swallowed so hard in my life. All that was missing was some bats flying around the top. And then I saw the bats.

Mazy pulled my head down and asked me if I was crazy. "She can't see *any* of us. Not until we spring our surprise," she said.

A bunch of the Mirror Queen's servants picked up the box and carried us up all these stairs. Right to the Mirror Queen's round chamber at the top of the tower.

"This is it, guys," whispered Mazy.

"I deduce that you must be holding your wand," whispered Marty.

"I don't think I ever held it as tight," whispered Mazy. Then she gripped my shoulder.

"Jeez," I whispered. "You been working out or something?" Marty gripped my other shoulder. "Okay, we're all set," said Mazy, "but just remember that even though the Mirror Queen will

look young and beautiful on the outside, she's actually five hundred years old… and all haggard and evil-looking on the inside. And the only reason she looks so good is because she's been stealing *you-know-what* from people for centuries."

It suddenly got really cold inside that box. "I deduce that we must be inside the Mirror Queen's chamber at the top of her tower," said Marty.

"And what makes you say that, dude?" I whispered through chattering teeth.

"It's said that her round chamber is as cold as her soul," said Mazy.

That's when we heard the Mirror Queen's voice. She sounded rich and spoilt. "Bring the box and lay it before me," she told whoever was carrying us. "There'd better be a fresh young wizard inside."

"The box was delivered from the prince not five minutes ago," said some dude.

"This is it," whispered Mazy. "And on three, we all stand and I'll freeze her before she knows what's happening. One, two… THREE!"

So we jumped up like three jack-in-the-boxes. The lid flew off and there she was, the Mirror Queen, sat on a throne in this chamber with mirrors all the way round it. Mazy wasn't wrong about her being easy on the eye, either: long, black, shiny hair and big, dark eyes. This Mirror Queen character was a real looker.

So, before she even had a chance to draw breath, Mazy pointed her wand and said, "Freeze-us-make-ice-statue-us!"

The Mirror Queen started giggling like she was four years old. "You were supposed to freeze her, not make her laugh at us," I told Mazy out of the corner of my mouth.

Mazy didn't answer. She couldn't. Because she was the one who'd been frozen! And Marty had been frozen, too!

The Mirror Queen stood up. "Why weren't you frozen by the reverse spell that I put on my chamber?" she said.

"Maybe because I'm just a regular dude!" I said.

"Maybe because I'm just regular dude, *Your Majesty!*" she said. Then she stepped down and started sniffing me like I stank or something.

I looked into her eyes and I knew what she was about to say. "Don't say it," I said.

"Don't say it, *Your Majesty!*" she said.

"Whatever. Just don't say it, Your Majesty."

She sniffed me again. And then she said it: "Extraordinary! And now I'm going to lap up all your extraordinary power!"

I knew if I let her do that, we'd be toast for sure. So I started shaking Mazy and telling her to snap out of it. Then I figured that even if she did snap out of it, her spells would be useless. They'd just be reversed right back at her.

The Mirror Queen was about to grab me. Then she was going to lap up my extraordinary powers… with the long, green tongue that had just lolled out of her mouth! I'm talking all the way down to her waist, dudes! "Hey! Hands off!" I said.

"Hands off, *Your Majesty!*" she said. Which isn't an easy thing to say when your tongue is long and green and lolling down to your waist. "Hold still while I lap up all that delicious magic and make myself look seventeen again!"

While she was telling me that, I jumped backwards out of the box and made for the door. Then I realised there wasn't just one door. There were like a *dozen* doors all around her round chamber. She started yelling for guards to seize me. And all the doors burst open and guards ran in. They had long staffs with pointy ends. So I dodged past three of them and made for a door. But a guard was standing in front of it. So I ran to a window and turned and yelled, "I'm just a regular dude! And this kind of stuff should not be happening to a regular dude!"

The Mirror Queen rose up in the air and hovered like she was wearing a jet-pack. Her green tongue was lolling all the way down to her feet now. "You are not a regular dude," she lolled at me. "You have extraordinary powers and I intend to gobble them all!"

That's when she cackled like some freaky old witch in a fairytale. Man, I looked out of the window, but that tower was *way* up in the air. So I'm standing there and thinking there's *no way* I can escape. And the cackling was getting closer and closer. It felt like I'd fallen right into a scary movie.

Then I muttered, "If only I had a remote control… I could switch channels… or pause her!" Right then I felt something in my hand: it was a remote control, dudes! And right smack-bang in the middle of the remote was a button with 'pause' written under it. So I spun about and pushed it right in that cackling face. And it wasn't just the cackling face and lolling tongue went all freeze-frame. It was all the guards in that tower room, too.

About a minute and a half of head-scratching later…

So about a minute and a half of head scratching later, I figured maybe if I pointed the remote at Mazy and hit the pause button again it might un-pause her. "Here goes nothing," I said, trying to un-pause Mazy.

"Arrrr!" cried Mazy, tumbling backwards out of the box. She landed with a crunch. "Ow! What just happened!?" she said.

"Well," I said, "as far as a regular dude can make out, you went and froze yourself and Marty, and then the Mirror Queen went and lolled her tongue at me like she was going lap up my extraordinary powers. So I magicked up this remote and used it to pause her and all the guards. And then I un-paused you and… Marty," I said, un-pausing Marty. The little detective dude tumbled backwards out of the box and landed beside Mazy. He looked like he'd just deduced a question.

"No time to explain," said Mazy, jumping to her feet. "We need to find the princess and rescue the entire school before Jimmy's pause spell wears off!"

"If it does, I can just pause her again."

"With what? Your *pinky* finger?" said Mazy. And that's when I realised that the remote had vanished. So we made off down the stone steps to the room below. No sign of the princess. Just a bunch of fancy dresses. We headed down to the room below that one. No sign of the princess. Just a bunch of fancy shoes. I guess as we made our way down that tower we found a bunch of rooms that had the Mirror Queen's stuff in them.

"I deduce that the princess is in a dungeon under the tower," said Marty, blowing bubble bars out of his pipe.

Several minutes and a lot of going down stairs later…

Several minutes and a lot of going down stairs later, we reached this big black door with a big, fat guard outside it. The dude was asleep on a chair. "I deduce that the sharp end of that guard's staff is sharp," said Marty. "And I further deduce that those keys on his belt will fit the dungeon door."

We huddled close to the guard and looked closely at the key and tried to figure out a way to get the key from the chain without waking him. That's when the guard opened his eyes and peered at us like wasn't expecting to see us – which was obviously a cue for Marty to make one of his brilliant deductions.

"I deduce that you weren't expecting to see us," he told the guard, whose eyes were about as wide as saucers. He was about to reach for his pointy staff when Marty whipped out a gold pocket watch.

"Anyone with a weak mind should look away now," said Mazy. I figured she couldn't mean me. So Marty started swinging the pocket watch in front of the guard's eyes.

"You're feeling very, very sleepy," he told him. And I'm thinking, he has *got* to be kidding, this guy looks *so* ready to stick two wizard kids and a regular dude with his pointy staff.

But the guard just said, "I'm feeling sleepy?" Then Marty said, "Yes, you are… very, *very* sleepy."

"Very, *very* sleepy?" said the guard.

"That's right," Marty told him. "And when I click my fingers, you will fall into a deep sleep." So Marty clicked his fingers.

A couple of minutes later…

A couple of minutes later I was lying on my back and someone was slapping my cheeks and saying, "Wake up!"

I opened my eyes. Marty and Mazy were leaning over me. "What happened, dudes?" I asked them.

"Hush! Keep your voice down or you'll wake the guard." Then Mazy held up the dungeon key and grinned at me.

Inside the princess's cell, we found the princess looking for something. She looked pretty much like you'd expect a fairytale princess to look: long, blonde hair all tied into a braid, big blue eyes, and she was wearing a purple princess outfit that made her waist look about two inches wide. She suddenly realised there were three other people in her cell with her. "I don't suppose you've seen it?" she asked us, like we hung out there all the time.

"Ah, *no*. We've come to rescue you, Your Highness," said Mazy.

"But if I could just find it I wouldn't need rescuing," she said, looking for something again. "Find what?" said Mazy.

"Why, my frog, of course," she said, clasping her hands together and going doe-eyed.

So I put my hand in front of my mouth and whispered, "She might be dangerous."

"Have you seen my frog?" she asked again, so doe-eyed that she'd almost gone boss-eyed.

"Yes! I've seen it!" said Marty, blowing bubble frogs out of his pipe.

As soon as the princess saw those bubble frogs she went into crazy overdrive and tried to catch them. She leaped in my direction and reached for a bubble frog by my head. She popped it against my head and her eyes opened real wide. "My prince! At last! I've found you! And now I know you will rescue me!"

"What? And *what*? Take a good look, fairytale princess chick. I'm like a foot shorter than your prince and fifteen years younger."

So she took a step back and had a good look. "Oh, my!" she said. "What horrible spell has that evil Mirror Queen placed on you? It's horrible!"

"Okay. Time out," I said. "I think she just insulted me."

"Oh, you *think*," said Mazy.

That's when the princess planted a kiss right on my smackers. Like I said, this fairytale princess was quite a looker. So it's not like I had much to complain about. At least, not until she said, "Why hasn't it worked? Is he to remain a giant, two-legged frog forever?"

"Double time out!" I said. "I'm not a giant, two-legged frog, lady. I'm actually a pretty cool dude *and* I have some pretty extraordinary powers. Go on. Tell her…" Suddenly all I could see is the princess's shoe. It looked the size of a car. So I tried to say, 'What the hey!?' but all I heard was a frog croak. And every time I tried to speak that frog croaked again. That's when I realised that that was no frog. It was me! The next thing I knew I was looking into this giant eye. I guess Marty was bending right over and peering at me through his magnifying glass. I knew it was coming. So I tried to put my fingers in my ears. But I had no fingers. Just frog's legs.

"I deduce that Jimmy has been turned into a frog," he said.

"Oh, my! Did I do that to him? Shrink him from a giant, two-legged frog into a little four-legged one?" said the princess.

"Of course! Everything is reversed in this dreadful place," said

Mazy.

"I deduce that we should make good our escape while the Mirror Queen and all her helpers are still frozen under Jimmy's extraordinary spell," said Marty.

2 minutes later…

So, two minutes later, Marty, Mazy and the princess were high-tailing it out of the haunted tower and into the woods. And I was hopping behind them.

"Stewie!" yelled Mazy. "Stewie!" she called again into the woods.

Suddenly, a window flew open at the top of the haunted tower. And the Mirror Queen stuck out her head. Man, did she look old and haggard now. Like she'd aged about five hundred years.

"What happened to her?" said the princess.

"She looks her age. The way she should look. It's what happens if she doesn't drain people of *you-know-what*… or wizards of their magic," said a voice I didn't recognise.

So I did a 180-degree hop and saw a frog behind me. "Man, I hope I'm not looking in a mirror," I croaked at it.

That was when Mazy yelled out, "Stop with all the croaking and leap up here!" So I did another 180-degree hop and saw that Stewie had turned up with his cart.

"Stop them!" cried the Mirror Queen from the top of her tower.

So I did another 180-degree hop. "Gotta go!" I told the frog. And then I did another 180-degree

hop.

"Oh no, you don't," croaked the frog, grabbing my back legs.

"Let go, frog dude! Is there like no honour amongst frogs?!"

"Forget honour! I want the reward!" he said, holding fast.

"What reward?" I said.

"There's always a reward!" he said, holding faster.

"A reward of a thousand gold coins for anyone who stops them!" said the Mirror Queen.

"Told you!" said the frog.

"But you're a frog, dude! What's a frog going to do with all that gold?"

"Lots of stuff. Buy my own pond. And fill it with lilies!"

Mazy called out, "For the love of magic, stop playing with your new froggie friend and jump on this cart!" That's right. She called that greedy frog dude my 'new friend'. I'd had enough. I really had. So I kicked that frog dude so hard that he went flying right through the door into the haunted tower. I guess having frog's legs can come in handy sometimes.

A second later…

A second later, I'd taken another jump at the cart. And I could see Marty's lips moving, which meant he was making a deduction. And from the look on his face, I deduced that he'd deduced how much I'd underestimated my frog's legs. Next thing I knew, I'd flown over the cart and landed in a bush on the other side. That's when we heard guards running down the haunted tower's winding staircase.

"Come on! I'll catch you," shouted Mazy, holding out her hands like I was a ball. I jumped… "Got him! Go!" Mazy told Stewie. So Stewie pulled away and headed off down the forest lane.

"We're out of the haunted tower," I croaked. "It's probably safe to use your wand now. So turn me back already."

"I think he's trying to tell me something," said Mazy, holding me up to her face.

"And he's turned a horrible shade of green."

"I'm a frog! You ever seen a frog that wasn't a horrible shade of green? Now turn me back already!" I croaked.

"I think he just asked to be his old self again," said Stewie.

"Oh, right!" said Mazy. She whipped out her wand.

"That won't work," Stewie told her as he cantered down the path. "There's only one way to turn a frog back into a person in these parts."

"Oh, yes? And how's that?" Mazy asked.

"You have to kiss him. On his lips."

"What!? Gross. Do frogs even *have* lips?" she said, staring at the place where a frog's lips should probably be. Boy, did she grimace. Then she handed me to the princess. "I believe this is your area of expertise, Your Majesty."

"If she caused the change in the first place, that won't work," said Stewie. "It has to be someone else."

"Oh, that's right…" said the princess, handing me back to Mazy. Boy, did the princess look relieved.

"Are you sure about this? I mean, I'm not a princess. And Jimmy Drummer is certainly no prince," said Mazy.

"Doesn't matter," Stewie said. "It's just the way of things in these fairytale parts."

I guess my feelings were a little mixed. I mean, a kiss on the smackers from Mazy was no bad thing. But I knew I had a serious problem: frog breath.

"Can't Marty do it?" said Mazy. Man, I was about ready to hop out of there. Spend the rest of my days as frog's spawn.

"No. It has to be the lips of a fair maiden," said Stewie.

So Mazy sighed and planted a smacker right on my lips. Suddenly, I was standing there dressed from head to toe in black velvet like a fairytale prince. Man, that dumb costume even had big silver buttons down the front. So I looked down at myself and muttered something about it being a good thing that no one back in my home town can see me now. And then I looked up to find myself standing in the mall in my home town! Man, it was so busy, it must have been a Saturday. "It's not Halloween, dude," some guy called out.

"I know that. Does this *look* like a Halloween costume?"

"You're right. I guess not. So what have you come to the mall dressed as, dude? The Prince of Uncool?" he said, high-fiving his two friends. They were laughing so much I thought they were going to choke to death. So I was about to give those dudes a piece of my mind when this hand appeared from nowhere, grabbed my lace collar, and yanked me back onto that cart.

"What just happened?" asked Mazy.

"You tell me," I said. "I was just thinking how good it was that no one in my home town could see me in this dumb costume… and then I was standing in the mall in my home town."

"Then it's obvious what you have to do to get us back to the school!"

"It is?"

"Yes! Maybe you should thank your lucky stars that we're NOT back at the school where Dave can see us looking so frightened and ridiculous!"

"Why should…" Man, the penny dropped so hard it could have broken my foot.

"Into the huddle!" said Mazy.

"I deduce that a plan is a-foot," said Marty, puffing feet from his bubble pipe.

That's when the Mirror Queen flew over us on her broomstick and landed on the path up ahead. She held out her hands and a ball of lightning started to fizz in them. "I'm going to fry you up and eat you all for breakfast!" Boy, did she look and sound like an old hag. And the ball of lightning in her hands was growing bigger and bigger.

"Do it, Jimmy!" said Mazy.

"Okay. Okay."

"And don't mess it up!" Right then her and Marty nodded at each other and grabbed my shoulders.

"Okay! I'm… I sure am glad that NO ONE at the Wizard School, KIDS OR TEACHERS, can see us looking so frightened right now…"

A second later…

A second later we were back at the wizard school, huddled up on a stage at one end of a humungous dining room. And that place was full to BURSTING with wizard kids and teachers. And they were all staring at us like we were some kind of huddling freaks.

"You've saved the day! You're a genius!" said Marty.

Mazy grinned at everyone like there was a perfectly reasonable explanation for all of this. And under her breath she said, "Let's not get carried away. It was *my* idea. But getting the whole school here was… well, I suppose it was a nice touch." That's when the teachers started blowing whistles and shouting for everyone to go back to their dorms and lock their doors. Man, talk about late to the party. The emergency was so over it was the opposite to sunny-side-up.

I'm back at my desk in my dorm now. And I really need a lie down. Professor Markus McDougall wants to see the three of us in his office first thing tomorrow morning. I'll let you know how all that goes in my next diary. And then there's the start of my first semester. Oh, yeah, I almost forgot… the fairytale princess will be sharing Mazy's dorm until we can find a way to get her back to her prince. I guess the Mirror Queen was so mad she closed all the borders between here and there. So until next time, take care of yourselves, dudes!

The end

Thank you for reading! If you enjoyed this book you might also enjoy *Jack Tracy & The Priory of Chaos: 2017 Edition* by the same author. The opening pages of which follow here.

Book description for *Jack Tracy & The Priory of Chaos: 2017 Edition*

For as long as he can remember, 12-year-old Jack Tracy has daydreamed about going on dangerous adventures just like the heroes of his books. And wondered if he truly possessed the courage of his daydreams. So, when Jack discovers that he's been chosen to travel to another realm to destroy the evilest school in all creation, he reasons he's about to find out one way or another. An incredible adventure is about to begin!

Prologue

On a leafy suburban street on the outskirts of London, in a place known to all the world as Wimbledon, there lived a 12-year-old boy called Jack Tracy.

The years that had delivered Jack to the cusp of his teens could best be summed up in one word: uneventful. Their highlights, if you could even call them such, where as follows: Jack's realisation that he *finally* had teeth enough to tackle solid food without serious risk of choking. His ability to stand on two legs as opposed to crawling around his playpen like a tortoise. And last but by no means least, the feeling of extraordinary freedom that his first stabilised bike had given him as he pedalled furiously around his little garden in search of a gap in the fence. Why the need for a gap? Jack longed to escape to the world of adventure that he had reliably been informed was chronicled truthfully in the pages of his books. Unable to find a gap, and as the years rolled on, Jack had only managed to escape to the school run, where he'd been forced to rely upon his extraordinary imagination for the adventures he craved.

This explains why Jack spent much of his time, spare or otherwise, as his mother liked to put it, 'Away with the fairies'. An unfair comment as during his bouts of day dreaming, Jack had not encountered a single fairy. You see, whenever Jack got his glassy-eyed, far *far* away stare, he was engaged in derring-do. And the more derring the do the better. And, like most children, in his more reflective moments, Jack seriously doubted that he possessed the courage of his daydreams. He wished he did with all his heart because the one thing that Jack liked to imagine above all else was protecting the kind of heart against tyrants and bullies.

And so it was, on a cold and windswept morning in February, soon after his twelfth birthday, that Jack Tracy was to discover if he truly possessed the courage of his daydreams ...

ONE

Jack Tracy's neighbourhood, 7.30am

"I don't want to go to school, Mum! It's too dangerous."

"Oh, now you're just being ridiculous, Anthony."

Anthony peered through a gap in the drawn living room curtains. "I'm not! They've gone now ... I *think*, I can't see them but you *must* have seen them when you went outside just now."

Anthony's mother shook her head. "All I saw was old Mr Grimshaw cleaning his car."

"*What*? One of the gang was *standing* on his car when you went out there! You're not blind ... you must have seen him!"

"No Anthony, I didn't. Now stop this nonsense. Do you hear me? This is *Wimbledon*. And there are no gangs in Wimbledon. Okay? Good boy. I have to go to work and *you* have to go to school. It's called *getting on with life*. What have I always told you?"

"That mother always knows best," murmured Anthony uncertainly.

"That's right. That mother always knows best. Now fetch your school bag and *go* to school."

Many cars had driven past Anthony's assault on Barton Road. But while children in their back seats gasped and pointed – their parents looked at the same street corner, and saw only a little girl playing hopscotch. Some children going to school on foot hurried past Anthony's ordeal, while others did 180s and sought safer routes. There was one exception: a 12-year-old boy with a pale face and spiky auburn hair stood transfixed across the street – his mouth fallen open, his nut-brown eyes wide in bafflement. A police car turned into the street. *Yes,* thought Jack Tracy, *the cavalry's here ...*

The police car pulled up. An officer climbed out of the driver's seat holding a letter. "Come on ... *do* something," muttered Jack. The policeman crossed the road to a letterbox, popped the letter inside, and strolled back to his car, whistling. As he climbed in and pulled the door closed, he noticed a boy staring at him.

"You'll catch flies in that mouth if you're not careful, son," said the officer.

Jack darted across the road and rapped on the car's window. The window whirred down. "Is there a problem, lad?"

"*What*? Are you joking? They're killing that guy!" said Jack, wincing at the sounds of Anthony's cries.

The policeman scratched the end of his nose and asked. "What guy?"

"That guy! There!" said Jack, pointing at the post box where the thugs now cheered every failed attempt to post Anthony's head. The policeman followed the tip of Jack's finger and saw only a little girl holding a letter – she smiled sweetly at him and posted it.

"I suppose you are aware that it's a criminal offence to wind up a police officer, son?" said the policeman, smiling at the girl.

Jack felt dizzy. "I can't believe this ... maybe I'm dreaming?" Jack took a step back from the car and stumbled slightly. *If this kid isn't a glue sniffer then I'm a monkey's uncle,* thought the policeman.

The squad car's engine purred into life. "I suggest you wake up young man ... or you'll be heading for a whole heap of trouble."

"Well, if you won't do anything about it ... I'll have to try," murmured Jack. The policeman pointed to his own temple and made a circular motion with his finger. The window whirred up.

Jack's heart pounded as he squeezed a path through the jeering bodies. He emerged beside Anthony. Anthony gazed up from the pavement into Jack's sympathetic face. His bloody lips parted and he said, "P ... please. I'm Anthony ... help me."

Jack felt that age old hatred of injustice surge within him, and he clenched his fists and bellowed "**WHY!**" towards the heavens.

Unbeknown to Jack, his question had travelled as far as his extraordinary imagination – to a place beyond human perception; to where even light from the brightest stars failed to reach.

And it had been heard.

Back on Barton Road, silence descended like a hangman's noose. A thug scratched his chin, narrowed his eyes at Jack and said, "Before we kill you kid ... why what?" Jack felt his anger slip away ... replaced by a terror that wrapped itself around his gut ... and squeezed. *I'm going to die now.*

The silence was shattered by a chirpy ring tone. A girl answered her phone. Her eyebrows furrowed, "Albion Street!" The gang scattered into the surrounding streets like rats.

Anthony gazed up at Jack like he was some kind of superhero. Jack looked over his own shoulder. "What? It wasn't me. They got a call."

TWO

Running the gauntlet

The following morning ...

In the alley that ran down the side of his house, a boy climbed onto Jack's garden fence and tumbled into his backyard. The gang out front had left him little choice. The boy sat in the vegetable patch, thinking.

Mrs. Tracy heard a 'tap tap tap' on the back door. *Must be Henry.* "I wish he'd just use the front door like everyone else." Mrs. Tracy drew a deep breath and opened the door. Henry Roscoe gazed at her with an expression of wide-eyed innocence. "You're right to look concerned, Mrs. T. It's bad news, I'm afraid. It looks as though you've got a *serious* mole problem."

Mrs. Tracy's hand went to a cluster of moles on her neck. "... *What?*"

Henry spoke up as though talking to someone hard of hearing. "Serious – mole – problem."

"I'm not deaf."

"Oh, right." Henry craned his neck to see what Mrs. Tracy was covering with her hand. He said, "I recommend dousing the infected area with rat poison. Or you could just hire a farmer with a shotgun ... they love blasting furry little moles. No need to *wince*, Mrs. T. It's quite painless."

The boy's gone mad.

"I mean ... *anything* that could tear up your tomato patch like that," he went on, brushing some dirt from his backside, "should be shot as soon as possible."

"Oh. I *see*."

Henry shook his head. "I'm just sorry I had to be the one to break the bad news."

Mrs. Tracy placed her hands on her hips. "Second time this week, isn't it?"

"I'm glad you appreciate my position, Mrs. T.," he said, squeezing past her. Mrs. Tracy returned to her kitchen and added 'tomatoes' to her shopping list.

"Still out there?" asked Henry, as he entered Jack's bedroom.

"They just left. They're *psychotic* ... they just dragged a couple of guys away. In broad daylight! It's only a matter of time before they kill

118

someone. Mum can't even see them. I don't think any adults can. They're untouchable." Jack turned and looked at his best friend. Henry was half a head taller than Jack and twice his width. Jack shoved his school tie into place. "Listen Henry, as soon as Samantha comes out, we'll join her okay? ... Make sure she gets to school in one piece."

Henry stroked his chins. "Interesting plan, Jack ... now if we can just find someone to make sure we do too ..."

"You managed to avoid them. Well done."

Henry nodded. "Unfortunately, your mother's tomatoes paid the ultimate price."

"Hedgehog?"

"Mole. Keep up. Big blighter too," said Henry, noticing a button on his shirt had popped.

Samantha closed her front door and gazed up at the sky: the blackest clouds *ever* stretched as far as she could see. "Wasn't it supposed to be *sunny* today?" she said, heaving her school bag onto her shoulder and walking down her drive.

"Sam's on the move," said Jack.

The boys trampled down the stairs side by side. "Guys! Take it easy! You've had no breakfast, Jack," said Mrs. Tracy, poking her head out of the kitchen.

"It's okay, Mum. I'll get something from the shop."

"Make sure you do, Jack."

"I'll make sure he does," said Henry, giving Mrs. Tracy the thumbs up.

Samantha's shoulder drooped under the weight of her bag. It held not only her school books but two fat petitions against animal cruelty. She smiled as the front door opposite burst open and Jack and Henry got momentarily *wedged* in it. They spilled out onto the driveway and shoved one another as they crossed the street. "Hey, Sam. Have you got bricks in that bag or something," said Henry, panting.

"Certainly feels like it," she replied.

"No problem. We've got the bag covered ..." said Henry, lifting it off her shoulder and handing it to Jack.

"Oh," said Samantha, "sure you don't mind?"

"I really don't," said Jack, only too pleased to take the weight off her slender shoulder. Samantha had dark wavy hair, clear pale skin and warm blue eyes.

She raised an eyebrow and said, "Thank God those cretins moved on. I told my mother about how they attacked that guy yesterday."

"And?" said Jack.

"And nothing. She accused me of exaggerating. God ... even by her standards the words 'head', 'bucket' and 'sand' have never been more appropriate."

Henry patted Jack's back. "Jack saved that guy's life."

"No, I didn't. They got a call. What's up with everyone? Even the policeman ignored what was happening."

Samantha shrugged. "I expect he had to fill in some forms back at the station."

Jack stopped in his tracks. "No, Sam. It was like he couldn't see it. It was happening right in front of him ... and he *couldn't* see it."

"I thought policemen were supposed to have 20/20 vision? Or is that fighter pilots?" mumbled Henry.

Samantha pulled a scary face. "All the adults have been placed under an enchantment and the world is being sucked into Hell, ha, ha, haaar."

Jack and Henry looked at her, horrified.

"*Metaphorically* speaking, guys. Lighten up."

They walked around a corner and spotted the gang standing under a tree. They were following the evasive manoeuvrings of a cat in its branches. A number of stones, empty bottles and bricks had been collected as missiles. "They're actually placing bets on who can knock it off that branch first," said Samantha, stepping towards them. Jack grabbed Samantha's arm. "Leave it, Sam. There's nothing we can do." Samantha grimaced as though she'd just heard the worst news *ever*.

The next moment, Jack heard himself say, "I suppose we could ... you know ... draw their fire or something. Give the cat a chance to get away."

"Are you nuts?" said Henry.

Must be, thought Jack.

"I always suspected you might be nuts and if you *insist* on this 'plan' then you'll just have confirmed my suspicions beyond any reasonable doubt and ..."

"Oh, stop babbling Henry! I think it's an excellent idea," said Samantha, her heart racing now. They were a stone's throw from the bus stop.

Jack went on, "If we time it just right, we could save the cat ...and maybe even ourselves." He looked for the number 23 coming along the high street.

"Oh, no ... there's a bus coming," said Henry, squinting into the distance. "Although ... let's not be hasty, it might be a Post Office van or ..."

"That's a bus and it's moving fast ... it's now or never." Before he could change his mind, he took a deep breath and yelled: "At least cats only catch rats! You cretins are evolving into them!"

The gang turned. A lanky thug pointed at Jack and said, "Isn't that the kid from yesterday? The one with a death wish?"

"Yes, it is. I say we grant him *and his mates* three death wishes," said another, taking aim with a broken bottle.

"Run!" croaked Jack. Jack and Samantha darted in the direction of the bus stop. Henry attempted to dart but could only manage an amble. Empty bottles and stones flew at them: the bottles smashing on the pavement, the stones zipping past with spiteful intent. Jack reached the bus stop first. The bus had just pulled up and opened its doors. An elderly man stepped down onto the pavement. A bottle shattered on the ground – and filled the turn-ups of his trousers with glass. The old man grinned and shook his leg as though he'd just remembered something funny. Jack didn't think his reaction at all funny. In fact, it chilled him to the bone.

Once Samantha was safely on board the bus, Jack began shouting words of encouragement at Henry. "Come on, Henry!" he yelled, followed by "WATCH OUT!" as a bottle skimmed Henry's head and exploded against a lamppost. Jack gave Henry a shove up onto the platform of the bus and climbed in behind him. The bus driver closed the doors behind them and drove off, oblivious to the commotion. The trio made their way past a number of anxious young faces and sat down at the rear of the bus. "Did you see that?" Jack panted. "That bottle landed *right* in front of the old guy and he didn't even flinch! He couldn't see it."

Several anxious looking children within earshot nodded. "The old-timer was probably just playing it cool?" said Henry, turning in his seat and gazing out the rear window.

Thank you for reading! If you enjoyed this sample, *Jack Tracy & The Priory of Chaos: 2017 Edition* is available in paperback from Amazon.

Printed in Great Britain
by Amazon